SPIKE HEELS

by Theresa Rebeck

SAMUEL FRENCH, INC.
45 WEST 25TH STREET   NEW YORK 10010
7623 SUNSET BOULEVARD   HOLLYWOOD 90046
LONDON   *TORONTO*

IMPORTANT BILLING AND CREDIT
REQUIREMENTS

All producers of SPIKE HEELS *must* give credit to the Author of the Play in all programs distributed in connection with performances of the Play and in all instances in which the title of the Play appears for purposes of advertising, publicizing or otherwise exploiting the Play and/or a production. The name of the Author *must* also appear on a separate line, on which no other name appears, immediately following the title, and *must* appear in size of type not less than fifty percent the size of the title type.

All producers of SPIKE HEELS must also provide the following credits in any production of the play:

> "This play was given a staged reading in New Voices '90 at the Ensemble Studio Theatre, New York City."

[The above credit must be provided until January 30, 1995.]

> "Produced in workshop by New York Stage and Film Company in association with the Powerhouse Theatre at Vassar, July, 1990."

The following credit must also be provided until July 4, 1997 on the credit page of all programs and in all advertising of similar billings of 1/4 page or larger in which full credits appear. The size of the billing is to be no smaller than the smallest creative element:

> "Original New York Production by The Second Stage Theatre on June 4, 1992."

Spike Heels was produced in workshop by New York Stage and Film Company in association with the Powerhouse Theatre at Vassar, July, 1990.

Spike Heels was originally produced in New York by the Second Stage Theatre on June 4, 1992. It was directed by Michael Greif and had the following cast (in order of appearance):

ANDREW ....Tony Goldwyn
GEORGIE......................... Saundra Santiago
EDWARD .... Kevin Bacon
LYDIA ....Julie White

Set Design: James Youmans
Lighting Design: Kenneth Posner
Costume Design: Candice Donnelly
Sound Design: Mark Bennett
Hair Design: Antonio Soddu
Production Manager: Carol Fishman
Production Stage Manager: Jess Lynn
Stage Manager: Allison Sommers

CHARACTERS

ANDREW

GEORGIE

EDWARD

LYDIA

TIME: The present

PLACE: Boston

ACT I

Scene 1

*Loud classical MUSIC, Vivaldi or Mozart, on the radio.
There is a long moment of POUNDING at the door.
LIGHTS come up on the main room of Andrew's
apartment, the orderly environment of a scholar.*

GEORGIE. (*Offstage.*) Andrew! Are you in there?
Dammit, goddammit, are you home, goddam you—
Andrew!

ANDREW. (*Overlapping offstage.*) Wait a minute—I'm
coming—

GEORGIE. (*Overlapping, offstage.*) Open up the
goddam door—are you home or WHAT—Jesus CHRIST I
am going to KILL myself I swear to God I will DAMMIT,
ANDREW!

*(ANDREW crosses the stage quickly, wiping his hands on
a towel, snaps off the radio and opens the door.)*

ANDREW. What, what, what—

(HE opens the door. GEORGIE barges in.)

GEORGIE. I have been on the stupid goddamn T for an
hour and a half, squished between four of the smelliest fat

men on earth, all of them with their armpits in my face, in high heels—Am I interrupting?

ANDREW. No, I was just making dinner. Lydia's coming over—

GEORGIE. Oh. I won't interrupt.—

ANDREW. You're not interrupting—

GEORGIE. (*Charging ahead.*) Goddammit, I hate heels. I have ruined my arches for the rest of my life just so a bunch of stupid men can have a good time looking at my fucking legs. (*SHE sits and takes off her heels.*)

ANDREW. Nice mouth. Very nice mouth.

GEORGIE. Oh, don't start. Don't even fucking start, okay? If I had a fucking car I wouldn't have to take the fucking T. Do you know how long I have been in transit? An hour and a half.

ANDREW. Edward let you off at 4:30? What, did he have a nervous breakdown or something?

GEORGIE. I hope so. I hope he totally loses his mind. I hope he has a vision of how useless his whole stupid life has been, and I hope he jumps out his spectacular little office window and into the fucking Charles River, that is what I hope.

ANDREW. Come on, he's not that bad.

GEORGIE. I wish I still smoked. Why the hell did I have to quit smoking? Do you have any cigarettes? How the hell are we supposed to survive in this stupid country without cigarettes? I mean, they invent this terrific little antidote to everything, *cigarettes*, and then after they get you hooked on it they tell you that it's going to kill you. And you know, the thing is, I think I'd rather be killed by cancer than by life in general. I really think that. (*SHE circles the room gingerly, trying to get some feeling back in her feet.)*

ANDREW. Are you going to tell me what happened?

GEORGIE. I threw a pencil at Edward, okay? He was getting on my nerves, so I said, fuck you, Edward, and I threw a pencil at him. (*SHE starts to laugh.*)

ANDREW. Oh, Jesus. Here. Give me your foot.

GEORGIE. Excuse me? I say I threw a pencil at Edward, and you say give me your foot? What is that supposed to mean? Are we having a conversation here, or is this like some sort of art film or what?

ANDREW. (*Crosses to the couch, throws her shoes aside and begins to massage her foot.*) No wonder you're in a bad mood. These shoes look like some sort of medieval torture device.

GEORGIE. Don't just throw those around, those cost a fortune. What are you—Andrew, excuse me, but what are you doing?

ANDREW. I'm massaging your foot. It's supposed to be soothing. Isn't it soothing?

GEORGIE. Yes, it's very—I don't know if soothing is what I would call this.

ANDREW. Supposedly the muscles in the foot are connected to almost every other part of your body. So it's important that your feet are always relaxed. That's why you're in a bad mood; you've been abusing your feet.

GEORGIE. That's not why I'm in a bad mood.

ANDREW. (*Pause.*) How's that?

GEORGIE. It's nice. It's very nice.

ANDREW. (*Pause. ANDREW looks up at her for a moment, and becomes suddenly awkward. HE quickly sets her foot down and moves to the kitchen.*) I better get to work on dinner.

GEORGIE. (*Watches him exit, then sits in silence for a moment.*) So how's Lydia?

ANDREW. (*Off.*) She's fine. Fine. She's good.

GEORGIE. Good. How's the wedding?

ANDREW. (*Off. Pause.*) Fine. It's still a ways off, so nobody's too hysterical yet.

GEORGIE. That's good.

ANDREW. (*Off.*) She wants to meet you.

GEORGIE. She does?

ANDREW. (*Off.*) Yeah. She's coming over for dinner later on. You should stick around. It really is ridiculous that you two haven't met.

GEORGIE. Yeah, that's ridiculous, all right.

ANDREW. (*Reenters, carrying a cutting board and vegetables.*) So can you stay?

GEORGIE. Right. She's gonna come over for some romantic little vegetable thing and find me. I'm sure. (*SHE starts to leave.*)

ANDREW. She said we should all go out sometime—

GEORGIE. Fine, we'll do that sometime.

ANDREW. Georgie—

GEORGIE. What? I'm all sweaty and gross. My shirt is sticking to everything and I stink. I can't meet Lydia smelling like a sewer. She'll faint or gag or something.

ANDREW. Don't start.

GEORGIE. I'm sorry. I'm just not up to it, okay?

ANDREW. So don't stay for dinner. She won't be here for another hour. Just stick around for a while.

GEORGIE. Look—these clothes are killing me. I need to go upstairs. I can come back tomorrow.

ANDREW. Go put on one of my t-shirts, they're in the top drawer of the dresser. Come on. You still haven't told me the details of your assault on Edward.

GEORGIE. Andrew—

ANDREW. There's some shorts in there, too.

GEORGIE. Oh, fuck.

(SHE heads off, peeling her jacket as she goes. ANDREW cleans, puts away his books, etc.)

ANDREW. *(Calling.)* You'll be fine. It's just going to take a little while to get used to it all. You know, actually, you're doing great. I talked to Edward last week, and he said you're the best secretary he's ever had. So you should just chill out and be nice to him. He's not that bad, and he likes you a lot. As a matter of fact, I think he has a crush on you. *(HE sees something on the coffee table, picks up a book and slams it down. HE takes the book to a small garbage can by his desk and knocks the dead bug off.)* These goddam bugs are invading my living room now. Did you ever get a hold of Renzella? I thought he was sending somebody over. *(Pause.)* Georgie?

GEORGIE. *(Off.)* You got a regular boudoir in here. Lydia's been lending you some of her clothes, huh?

ANDREW. Hey, leave that stuff alone. *(Pause.)* Georgie?

GEORGIE. *(Off.)* I don't want to wear one of your t-shirts. I want to wear this. *(SHE appears in the doorway, wearing an elegant patterned silk dress. SHE slinks into the room.)*

ANDREW. I asked you not to start.

GEORGIE. Thank you. I picked it up at Saks. Usually I don't appreciate his line, but when I found this I was just devastated—

ANDREW. Take off the dress. Take it off now.

GEORGIE. I particularly like the bow.

ANDREW. I don't find this funny.

GEORGIE. I just thought I could pick up some fashion tips. So I look presentable when we all go out to dinner.

ANDREW. *This is not funny.*

(Pause.)

GEORGIE. Okay. It's not funny. Fine. (*Pause.*) I didn't mean anything. I just meant—this is a nice dress. Silk, huh? Lydia's kind of loaded, huh? (*Pause.*) You think this looks good on me? I mean, I got some money coming in now, maybe I should try to dress better.

ANDREW. I think you should take it off.

GEORGIE. Yeah. I guess I look pretty stupid. (*SHE crosses back to the bedroom.*)

ANDREW. I'm sorry. That's her favorite dress. I just— you don't even know her. She's nothing like that.

(GEORGIE exits.)

ANDREW. (*Calling.*) We'll set up a date this week and actually do it: we'll go out to dinner. The three of us. You two can spend the evening trashing Edward. It'll be fun. You'll be thick as thieves by dawn.

GEORGIE. (*Off.*) She doesn't like him either, huh?

ANDREW. Both of you, you're both heartbreakers.

(GEORGIE reenters and stands in the doorway, without her shirt on, wearing a slip and a bra. SHE carries the t-shirt in her hands.)

GEORGIE. What is that supposed to mean?

ANDREW. Nothing. I told you, I think he has a crush on you. I talked to him last week, and—

GEORGIE. You talked to him? You talked to him. What did he say?

ANDREW. Georgie.

GEORGIE. What?

ANDREW. Put your shirt on.

GEORGIE. *(Puts the t-shirt on. It is long and loose, with sleeves and neck cut out. When she pulls it over her shoulders, her breasts are still largely exposed. ANDREW points it out to her.)* You talked to him?

ANDREW. I talk to him all the time. You know that.

GEORGIE. So what did he say?

ANDREW. He said he liked you.

GEORGIE. Great. That's just—and what did you say?

ANDREW. I said I liked you, too.

GEORGIE. That's what you said? You said, "I like her, too." That's all you said?

ANDREW. *(Perplexed.)* Yes. That's all I said.

(Pause.)

GEORGIE. Great. Well, you know, as far as I'm concerned, Edward can just go fuck himself. I mean, your little friend is just a prince, isn't he? He's just a delight. *(SHE goes back into the bedroom.)*

ANDREW. (*Calling.*) Look—he hired you. You didn't have any references, you didn't have any legal experience, you didn't have a college degree. And he didn't ask any questions. You might think about that.

GEORGIE. (*Reenters, carrying a pair of gym shorts. While she speaks, SHE takes off her slip and pantyhose.*) Oh, I might, might I? All right. I'm thinking about that. Nothing is coming to me, Andrew. What is your point here?

ANDREW. My point is, he gave you a job. I'm not saying the man is a saint. But he gave you a job.

GEORGIE. Yeah, right, he "gave" me the damn job. I fucking work my ass off for that jerk; he doesn't give me shit. I earn it, you know? He "gave" me the job. I just love that. What does that mean, that I should be working at McDonald's or something, that's what I really deserve or something?

ANDREW. You wouldn't last two hours at McDonald's. Some customer would complain about their French fries and you'd tell him to fuck off and die, and that would be the end of that.

GEORGIE. Bullshit. Fuck you, that is such fucking bullshit. You think I don't know how to behave in public or something?

ANDREW. (*Overlap.*) Georgie—could you put your clothes on—Georgie—

GEORGIE. (*Ignoring him, overlapping.*) Jesus, I was a goddam waitress for seven years, the customers fucking loved me. You think I talk like this in front of strangers; you think I don't have a brain in my head or something? That is so fucking condescending. Anytime I lose my temper, I'm crazy, is that it? You don't know why I threw that pencil, you just assume. You just make these assumptions. Well, fuck you, Andrew. I mean it. Fuck you. (*SHE takes her clothes in her hands and heads for the door.*)

ANDREW. You can't go out in the hall like that—

GEORGIE. I mean, I just love that. You don't even know. You've never seen me in that office. You think I'm like, incapable of acting like somebody I'm not? For four months I've been scared to death but I do it, you know, I take messages, I call the court, I write his damn letters. I watch my mouth, I dress like this—whatever this is; these are the ugliest clothes I have ever seen—I am gracious, I am bright, I am promising. I am being this other person for them because I do want this job but there is a point beyond which I will not be fucked with! So you finally push me beyond that point, and I throw the pencil and now you're going to tell me that that is *my* problem? What, do you guys think you hold all the cards or something? You think you have the last word on reality? You do, you think that anything you do to me is okay, and anything I do is fucked because I'm not using the right words. I'm, like, throwing pencils and saying fuck you, I'm speaking another language, that's my problem. And the thing is—I am America. You know? You guys are not America. You think you are; Jesus Christ, you guys think you own the world. I mean, who made up these rules, Andrew? And do you actually think we're buying it?

(*Pause.*)

ANDREW. Maybe you should sit down and tell me what's going on.

GEORGIE. Yeah, and maybe you should go fuck yourself. (*Pause.*) I'm sorry, okay?

ANDREW. Are you okay?

GEORGIE. Yes! No. Christ. I'm sorry. I'm sorry.

(*Pause. THEY stand for a moment in silence. ANDREW crosses and puts his arm around her. SHE leans against him.*)

ANDREW. What happened at the office?

GEORGIE. I don't know. You got anything to drink around here? I mean, could I have a drink?

ANDREW. Do you want some tea?

GEORGIE. Tea? Are you kidding? I mean, is that supposed to soothe me or something? I hate to break the news to you, but I really think that that is like, just a myth, Andrew. I think that in reality vodka is far more soothing than tea.

ANDREW. I don't have any vodka.

GEORGIE. Bourbon works too.

ANDREW. I have half a bottle of white zinfandel.

GEORGIE. Oh, Jesus. Make me tea.

(*HE exits to the kitchen. GEORGIE crosses, picks up the gym shorts and puts them on. ANDREW reenters.*)

ANDREW. All right. Now tell me what happened.

GEORGIE. Nothing happened. I mean, it's stupid.

ANDREW. (*Pause.*) That's it? It's stupid? You can talk for hours about absolutely nothing, and now all you have to say about something that is clearly upsetting you is, it's stupid?

GEORGIE. I feel stupid.

ANDREW. What are you talking about, you feel stupid? You just walked in here and insulted me for ten minutes.

GEORGIE. That was different. I was mad.

ANDREW. You have to be mad to talk?

GEORGIE. No, come on—I don't know—

ANDREW. I could make you mad.

GEORGIE. No, you couldn't. You're too nice.

ANDREW. Fuck you.

GEORGIE. —Andrew—

ANDREW. Fuck you. Come on. Fuck you.

GEORGIE. (*Calm.*) Yeah, fuck you too.

ANDREW. Fuck you.

GEORGIE. Fuck you.

ANDREW. Fuck you.

GEORGIE. You look really stupid saying fuck you—

ANDREW. Fuck you. Fuck you! Fuck you.

GEORGIE. (*Laughing. Overlap.*) Andrew, stop it. Cut it out. It sounds weird when you say it. You shouldn't talk like that.

ANDREW. You talk like that all the time!

GEORGIE. I'm different. I mean, I know how to swear. You don't. It's like, fuck you. Fuck you. Or, you know, fuck you. It's just—you know. You got to know how to say it.

ANDREW. Fuck you.

GEORGIE. Forget it. You look really stupid. You look the way I look when I try to talk like you.

ANDREW. You've tried it? Really? I must have missed that day.

GEORGIE. Oh, fuck you. You know I can do it; I can be as snotty and polite as anybody and it just makes me look stupid.

ANDREW. Georgie, it doesn't. You just—look. The English language is one of the most elegant and sophisticated languages on earth, and it will let you be whatever you want. If you use it carefully, and with respect, it can teach you things, it will allow you to uncover thoughts and ideas you never knew you were capable of; it will give you access to wisdom. Sophistication. Knowledge. Language is a gift that humanity has given itself to describe the world within, and without, with grace and wonder, and you can do that. Or you can use it badly and just be what you say you are. You can just be a, a fucking—cunt, if that's all you ever—

GEORGIE. UGGH. I can't believe you used that word. Oh, my God. You should see these words coming out of your mouth. It's so fucking weird. I'm not kidding, Andrew. I wouldn't swear if I was you.

ANDREW. Forget it. (*The tea kettle WHISTLES.*) You want that fucking tea?

GEORGIE. No. I don't want the fucking tea.

ANDREW. (*Exits to the kitchen and turns off the kettle. HE re-enters.*) You want to tell me what happened?

GEORGIE. Oh, God. It really is stupid. I mean, what do you think happened? He wants to screw me is what happened.

(*Pause.*)

ANDREW. Could you elaborate on that?
GEORGIE. What, you don't know what that means?

ANDREW. He propositioned you or he tried to rape you or what? You have to be more specific; "screw" covers a lot of ground.

GEORGIE. Well, in his own weird little way he tried both, okay?

ANDREW. (*Pause.*) Georgie, don't kid around with me now—

GEORGIE. Just sit down, Andrew. He didn't lay a hand on me, he just—Look. Last week he tells me we have to talk about my future with the firm so we go out to dinner and he tells me how amazing I am and I could be a paralegal if I keep this up. I spilled my soup, I got so excited. So then he took me home and asked if he could come up, and I said sorry, but I would like to keep our relationship professional. See, I do know how to talk like you assholes when I want to, so you can just stop acting like I'm a fucking idiot with words.

ANDREW. So he propositioned you.

GEORGIE. Last week, that was last week. Yesterday, he has me stay late, right? He says, "Georgie, could you stay late and type up some interrogatories." And I say, "sure." Then after everybody's gone he invites me into his office and asks me if I knew his couch folds out into a bed. So I say, "I have to get to work, Edward." But he wants to have a debate about the pros and cons of whether or not I should screw him. It was amazing, it went on for twenty minutes, I am not kidding. So I finally said, "Edward, I don't have to debate this with you. I don't have to be polite, you know? I'm not going to fuck you." So he says, he doesn't have to be polite either and he could just rape me if he wanted because everybody else is gone and the security guard isn't due until ten. And I stared at him—and, you know, I could see it in his little lawyer's face; he could've done it. (*Pause.*) I mean, on the one hand, it was no big deal; I just walked out of the office and took the stairs, 'cause I wasn't going to wait for any elevator. I mean, I was scared, but I didn't think he was going to do anything because it was pretty clear that in his own sick little mind, just saying it was as good as doing it.

ANDREW. You went to work today? You went to work after that?

GEORGIE. That job means a lot to me! (*Pause.*) What was I supposed to do, just quit and go back to—fuck, I don't know—I mean—I don't want to go back and be a waitress! What was I supposed to do? Quit because Edward is an asshole? I didn't care, I didn't think he'd try it again! I didn't; I thought that was it!

ANDREW. Wasn't it?

GEORGIE. Today, he comes out of his office at about 4:30 and asks me to stay late to type a pleading. And he kind of looks at me, you know? So I said, fuck you, Edward, and threw my pencil at him.

ANDREW. (*Pause.*) Why didn't you tell me? Dammit. Why didn't you tell me last night?

GEORGIE. He said something, it was something he said.

ANDREW. He said something *worse*?

GEORGIE. No. No. It was just talk. You know? It was just talk. I just—I didn't want to make a big deal about it.

ANDREW. It *is* a big deal. It's indecent. It's a big deal. (*HE paces angrily.*)

GEORGIE. Andrew. You're mad. I've never seen you mad.

ANDREW. Yes, I'm mad! I'm mad! We'll sue him for harassment. We'll take him to court.

GEORGIE. What, are you kidding? He'll kill us. He's a really good lawyer.

ANDREW. I don't care. Dammit. Goddammit!

GEORGIE. You want some tea?

ANDREW. NO, I—(*Pause.*) I'm sorry. I shouldn't be yelling at you.

GEORGIE. It's okay. I mean, he didn't really do anything. It was just talk. Okay? Let me make you some tea.

(*SHE goes into the kitchen. ANDREW prowls the room angrily for a moment, then picks up the phone and dials. GEORGIE reenters with the tea.*)

GEORGIE. Andrew, what are you doing? You're not calling him, are you? Don't call him, okay? Andrew. I mean it.

ANDREW. (*Into phone.*) Hi, Jennine, it's Andrew. Can you see if Edward is still there?

GEORGIE. (*Overlap.*) Andrew, I'm not kidding. Could you put the—would you put the fucking receiver down? Oh, FUCK.

(*SHE crosses and pulls the cord out of the wall. THEY stare at each other for a moment, startled.*)

GEORGIE. What, did you think I was kidding? Did you not understand that I was saying I do not want you calling that asshole? Do you not understand English?

ANDREW. (*Picks up the ends of the phone cord, angry.*) Have you lost your mind?

GEORGIE. No, I have not lost my mind! What the fuck kind of question is that? I asked you nicely to put the phone down. It was your little macho choice to keep on dialing, so don't go acting like I'm insane. I just don't want you talking to him right now! I don't need you doing some sort of protective male thing here! Just for a minute, okay?

(*Pause.*)

ANDREW. Okay.

GEORGIE. I'm sorry about your phone.

ANDREW. It's okay.

GEORGIE. I'll get you another one.

ANDREW. It's okay.

GEORGIE. God, I should just go home before I make everything worse—

ANDREW. No. It's okay. I'm sorry, okay?

(*HE takes her face in his hands for a moment; SHE pulls away nervously.*)

GEORGIE. Okay. Let's talk about something else. Here's your tea. Chop those vegetables. Let's talk about— books. That'll cheer you up.

ANDREW. Georgie—

GEORGIE. No, come on, you're always beating me over the head to talk about books. I finished that one you gave me.

(SHE pulls a book out of her purse. THEY talk nervously.)

ANDREW. Already?

GEORGIE. It was good; it was a good read, you know? Reminded me of, like, Sydney Sheldon.

ANDREW. *The Iliad* reminds you of Sydney Sheldon. Great.

GEORGIE. Yeah, a lot happened, it would make a great mini series, you know? We should try the idea out on my sister; she's like the expert on junk TV. No shit, she lies around this apartment in the Bronx all day. .... What else you got?

(SHE picks up a book from the table. HE takes it from her.)

ANDREW. No, you can't have that. I'm using that.

GEORGIE. Oh. Right. Right! How's your book coming?

ANDREW. It's fine.

GEORGIE. You should let me help you with that. I mean, I'm out of work now. I could come down and plug it into your computer for you. No kidding, I'm fast. I'll type it up for you; you'll be done in a week.

ANDREW. Right.

GEORGIE. I could, I could help! I mean, as long as you're going to do this Pygmalion thing, you might as well get something out of it.

ANDREW. Do what?

GEORGIE. Isn't that what it's called? I heard Edward— uh—you know, I heard That Guy we both can't stand right

now tell one of the partners you were doing this pig thing.
So I asked Donna about it. Some guy wrote a whole book;
I bought it.

ANDREW. George Bernard Shaw.

GEORGIE. Yeah. I mean, it didn't exactly hit me as
being the same thing here—

ANDREW. It's not the same thing. It's not the same
thing at all. Edward doesn't know shit, okay? (*HE takes the
vegetables into the kitchen.*)

GEORGIE. (*Calling.*) Well—okay, he doesn't know
shit, but I thought there were similarities.

ANDREW. (*Reenters with wash cloth and begins
wiping off coffee table.*) It's not the same thing.

GEORGIE. Then what is it? (*Pause.*) I mean it. What is
this?

ANDREW. What is what?

GEORGIE. This. This. All the dinners and the books
and the lessons and the job. What is this, anyway? We
been doing this for like, six months or something, you
know? I mean—what's going on here, Andrew?

ANDREW. Georgie. We can take him to court.

GEORGIE. NO. I'm not talking about him. I'm talking
about this. What is this?

ANDREW. It's—friendship.

GEORGIE. Friendship.

ANDREW. Yes.

GEORGIE. You're sure about that.

ANDREW. Yes.

GEORGIE. You get that mad whenever anybody fucks
around with your friends, huh?

ANDREW. Yes.

(SHE looks at him. Suddenly, SHE crosses and sits very close.)

ANDREW. What are you doing?

GEORGIE. Nothing.

ANDREW. Georgie—

GEORGIE. I'm not doing anything. I'm just sitting next to my friend here with hardly any clothes on.

ANDREW. Come on. Don't do this. Please?

GEORGIE. Just once, Andrew. Don't you want to try it just once? Really. Don't you, kind of?

ANDREW. I don't think a one night stand is what you're looking for.

GEORGIE. Fine. We'll do it twice. She'll never know.

ANDREW. She's not the one I'm worried about. Georgie—oh, boy. Look, you're upset about what happened with Edward—

GEORGIE. Do I look upset?

ANDREW. But this isn't going to fix that—

GEORGIE. I don't need to be fixed. Come on, Andrew, let's just do it today. I had a bad day. I'm not upset—but I had a bad day.

ANDREW. Georgie—no—If I—I would be just as bad as him if I—I'm not going to take advantage of you like that.

GEORGIE. Fuck, yes, take advantage of me. Please. Don't be noble, Andrew. For once, don't be noble.

ANDREW. Georgie, sweetheart—

GEORGIE. Andrew. She's going to be here in half an hour. We don't have a lot of time to talk about this.

*(SHE slides her arms up around his neck. Protesting, HE
tries to pull her away. SHE resists and THEY wrestle
for a moment; ANDREW finally gets her turned around
and holds her in front of him with her arms crossed
under his.)*

GEORGIE. Okay, okay, if you don't want to, just say
so—
ANDREW. It's not that I don't want to! *(Pause.)* I want
to, all right?
GEORGIE. You do?
ANDREW. Yes. Oh, yes.

*(HE buries his face in her hair for a moment. SHE waits,
uncertain.)*

GEORGIE. Okay. *(Pause.)* Are we waiting for
something?
ANDREW. It's not that simple.
GEORGIE. Trust me on this one. It is that simple.

(SHE pulls away; HE holds her.)

ANDREW. Not fifteen minutes ago, you were on a
rampage; you were ready to murder me and every other man
you've ever met. Now you want to make love?
GEORGIE. Sex is kind of spontaneous that way.
ANDREW. It's not what you want.
GEORGIE. I'm pretty sure it is.
ANDREW. Please. Listen to me. Will you please
listen?

(SHE nods. HE releases her. Pause.)

ANDREW. All right. Nietzsche talks about the myth of eternal return.

GEORGIE. Oh, come on. Don't do this to me—

ANDREW. Thomas Hardy, historical repetition.

GEORGIE. Don't do this to me, Andrew—we don't have much time here!

ANDREW. *(Overlap.)* What history teaches is that people have never learned anything from history. Hegel. History is a nightmare from which I am trying to escape. James Joyce.

GEORGIE. *(Overlap.)* This is your fucking book. I don't want to hear about your stupid book now!

ANDREW. You better want to hear about it, because I'm not talking about my stupid book, I'm talking about your life. Historical repetition. One man treats you bad so you fall in bed with another. God. The system eats up people like you; you end up in dead end jobs, crummy apartments, bad neighborhoods, too many drugs, too much alcohol, meaningless relationships. They don't give you anything to live for, so you live for nothing! The complexities of what happens to the underclasses are so byzantine no one can make head or tail out of them anymore, we never could. We spin our theories, one after another, and it never amounts to anything; century after century we lose half the human race, more than half, to what? And why? I just didn't want to see you become a statistic.

GEORGIE. What does this have to do with whether or not we go to bed?

ANDREW. I will not become just another one of your lovers. We're both worth more than that.

GEORGIE. I didn't mean—

ANDREW. Relationships *mean* something. People *mean*. You don't sleep with every person you're attracted to; that's not the way it works. And aside from the crucial fact that I'm not about to betray Lydia, whom I love, I'm not going to betray you. You want to know what this is? I am not your friend, okay? I am your teacher. And you don't sleep with your teacher; it screws up everything. You don't do it.

GEORGIE. Fine. Okay, fine. I mean, I just wanted to sleep with you. I didn't mean to threaten world history.

ANDREW. Georgie. It's not that I don't want to.

GEORGIE. No, it's fine, I don't care, I shouldn't of— I'm no better than Edward, am I?

ANDREW. No. You are.

GEORGIE. What's Lydia like? Is she like you? I mean, is she gentle, like you?

ANDREW. I guess so.

GEORGIE. Edward is so full of shit. You know, he told me—He told me the reason he came on to me was because you told him to.

ANDREW. What?

GEORGIE. Yeah. I mean, I didn't believe him. Because it was so creepy, and you're not—I mean, you're so Not That, but it just made me sick to hear it, you know?

ANDREW. (*Pause.*) What did he say?

GEORGIE. I don't know. He said you told him I was on the make or something and he should—you know? Then today when I got here, you said you talked to him, so

I thought—I mean, I didn't want to think it, but—I'm sorry. I just—I got freaked out. I'm sorry.

ANDREW. It's okay.

GEORGIE. What a creep.

ANDREW. Yeah. (*Long pause.*) It's getting late. We should—get going on this dinner.

(*HE picks up the dish rag and crosses to the kitchen. SHE watches him for an awful moment.*)

GEORGIE. (*Quiet, filled with dread.*) Andrew?

ANDREW. What?

GEORGIE. What did you say to him?

ANDREW. What?

GEORGIE. (*Pause.*) Oh, no. When I got here you said you talked to him. What did you say?

ANDREW. I said—I liked you. That was all I said.

GEORGIE. That was all?

ANDREW. Yes! I mean, no, I—of course, we talked about other things, but it wasn't anything—it wasn't—

GEORGIE. Why are you getting so nervous?

ANDREW. I'm not nervous! I'm trying to remember the conversation. He said—he wanted to ask you out, and I said I thought that would be okay. I told him you might be—I told him I thought you might need someone in your life, you seemed—Look. I thought you were getting a kind of a crush on me, so it might be good for you—

GEORGIE. You gave me to him?

ANDREW. No. That's not why I did.

GEORGIE. What the fuck would you call it? Why was he asking your permission to go out with me in the first place? Am I like your property or something and he has to get your permission—

ANDREW. Georgie, no; it was a misunderstanding. He thought there was something going on between us and he just wanted to know—

GEORGIE. Something going on. Some *thing*, huh? Christ, Andrew. I am in love with you.

ANDREW. (*Pause.*) I'm sorry. I didn't know.

GEORGIE. You didn't know? How could you not know?

ANDREW. Please, believe me, if I had known, I never would have said—

GEORGIE. You never would have said what? You never would have said, go ahead, take her? You never would have said that, huh? I can't believe you. You—you're just the same as the rest of them, aren't you? (*SHE picks up her bag and goes to the door quickly, furious.*)

ANDREW. No! That's not—Georgie, you're upset, you're not being fair, you're not thinking—

GEORGIE. Don't talk to me about fair, just don't even start!

ANDREW. Don't walk out. We have to talk about this. Georgie—

(*HE grabs her elbow. SHE shoves him hard. THEY stare at each other.*)

GEORGIE. Fuck that, Andrew. You don't like my language, and I don't like yours. I'm sick of talking, you know? You know what I mean? You guys—for all you know, you don't know shit. (*SHE exits.*)

BLACKOUT

Scene 2

Again, loud classical MUSIC on the radio; this time something more sinister—Stravinsky, Rachmaninoff. A bottle of scotch with a significant dent in it stands on the coffee table. KNOCKING on the door. After a moment, ANDREW crosses into the room.

ANDREW. Yeah, yeah, I'm coming—

(HE opens the door; EDWARD enters. ANDREW stares at him, aghast.)

EDWARD. Hi. How's it going?

ANDREW. Edward.

EDWARD. Nice. Nice welcome. Listen, your security's great here; your front door is wide open.

ANDREW. Edward, what are you doing here?

EDWARD. I'm returning your calls. Sorry I didn't get back to you; I was in court all day. Anyway, I'm supposed to have dinner with Georgie, so I thought I'd kill two birds with one stone. I won't stay.

ANDREW. *(Quietly astonished.)* What? You what?

EDWARD. Christ, what a day I've had. Can I use your phone? *(HE dials.)*

ANDREW. She's having dinner with you?

EDWARD. Yeah. Can you turn that down?

(ANDREW crosses to the MUSIC and snaps it off. EDWARD speaks into the receiver.)

EDWARD. Georgie. It's Edward. (*Pause.*) No, no, I'm in the building. I'm at Andrew's. So, can you just meet me down here? (*Pause.*) Hello? (*Pause.*) No, I just—Andrew wanted to talk to me about something, so I—No, I just got here. (*Pause.*) It's okay—okay, take your time. (*Pause.*) Okay, great. Bye. (*HE stares at the receiver, perplexed, and hangs up.*) Christ. You have anything to drink around here?

ANDREW. You're not staying.

EDWARD. (*Finds the bottle of scotch.*) Is this *scotch*? Andrew, congratulations. You learned how to drink scotch. (*HE exits to the kitchen, delivers part of his speech there, reenters pouring scotch and sits.*)

ANDREW. Edward—

EDWARD. (*Calling.*) You would not believe the day I've had. I spent the entire afternoon in front of McGilla Gorilla trying to convince her that three Jamaican dope peddlers with a collective list of priors as long as the Old Testament had been denied their rights. Some of these judges—I mean, I didn't write the fucking constitution. It wasn't my idea to give everybody rights. That was our founding fathers, remember? If she doesn't like it, she can complain to the goddam supreme court. The stupid cop violated their rights. He pulls them over—get this, the cop pulls them over because they ran a red light—and they all get into an argument, so he pulls a search and seizure and finds six pounds of marijuana in the trunk. Marijuana, okay, we're not even talking cocaine. And can you show me probable cause in an argument about whether the light was yellow or red? Can you do that for me, please? Four hours I'm arguing this shit. I mean, I got assigned this crummy case; someone give me a fucking break! I hate this pro bono shit. If I'm going to defend criminals I really prefer that they have lots and lots of money.

ANDREW. (*Crosses and takes the glass from him politely. Quiet.*) Don't make yourself at home; you're not staying. I've been calling you all day to let you know that I want you to stay away from her. If you ever go near her again, I'll have you charged with assault. No. Forget that. If you go near her, I'll cut your throat out. Do you understand? Now get out.

(Pause.)

EDWARD. Well. That was aggressive. You want to tell me what this is about?

ANDREW. You know what this is about.

EDWARD. Well, no, really, I don't, but I can make some wild guesses. You talked to Georgie?

ANDREW. Yes. I talked to Georgie.

EDWARD. She told you about the fight we had, huh?

ANDREW. Actually, what she told me was that you threatened to rape her.

EDWARD. What? Oh, that is not—

ANDREW. Don't. Just don't even try to talk your way out of this one. You know, frankly, I never thought even you could sink this low. Christ, we've been friends for what, fifteen years, and I've seen you go through a lot of women and I'm not always crazy about the way you treat them, but this—if anyone had asked me, I would've said, no, he's bad but he's not that bad—

EDWARD. (Overlap.)	ANDREW.
Andrew.	I didn't threaten her. I did not threaten her. Okay?

ANDREW. Spare me—

EDWARD. To the best of my recollection, in this country the accused is innocent until proven guilty, so can you give me a second here to tell you what happened?

ANDREW. Fine. Fine. Go right ahead.

EDWARD. Can I have my drink back, please?

(ANDREW looks at him, hands him the drink.)

EDWARD. I'm glad to see you're bringing an open mind to this. Okay. You want to know what happened? I came onto her. I admit it. That's not a crime; she's an attractive woman. And as you'll recall, I told you about this ahead of time; I got clearance from you, pal.

ANDREW. Don't throw that at me—

EDWARD. (*Overlap.*) I asked you—

ANDREW. (*Overlap.*)—You said you wanted to start seeing her!

EDWARD. Did you think that meant I was going to take her on a picnic?

ANDREW. I certainly didn't think it meant rape.

EDWARD. Oh, for—Nothing happened! I came onto her and she wasn't interested and I got mad. That's it. I got mad.

ANDREW. What did you say to her?

EDWARD. Please. Who remembers? It turned into a huge fight. The woman is screaming at me. I know very little.

ANDREW. What did you say?

EDWARD. Andrew—this woman makes Godzilla look like a Barbie doll.

ANDREW. What did you say?

EDWARD. I don't remember the specifics of the fight.

ANDREW. You did it, didn't you? You said it.

EDWARD. I did not threaten her, okay? I mean, we were having an argument, a discussion in my office, and I said some things that perhaps I should not have said, but I did not threaten her—

ANDREW. (*Overlapping.*) Oh, what, "some things that I should not have said," like I could just rape you—

EDWARD. All right, yes, perhaps I said that, that is not the same thing—

ANDREW. That's it. Get out.

(HE grabs at the drink. EDWARD resists and the scotch goes flying, covering both of them.)

EDWARD. Do you think we can discuss this like rational adults?

ANDREW. No, as a matter of fact, I don't think we can.

EDWARD. When I walked in, you said you wanted to slit my throat. That doesn't mean you'd actually do it, does it?

ANDREW. Oh, it might.

EDWARD. I was having a fight with my secretary, Andrew. We both said things we shouldn't have said. *(EDWARD turns away and goes to the kitchen. HE returns a moment later with a towel. HE dries himself off and throws it at Andrew.)*

ANDREW. It wasn't a fight. It was sexual harassment.

EDWARD. Oh, don't even say those words. Everyone's so fucking sensitive these days—

ANDREW. (*Overlap.*) I don't give a damn what you—

EDWARD. (*Overlap.*) As a term, "sexual harassment" is so overdefined it's almost meaningless. MacKinnon notwithstanding, at no point did I actually threaten her; and at no point did I suggest that her job security would be endangered by a failure to participate in a sexual act—

ANDREW. (*Overlap.*) Shut up. WOULD YOU PLEASE SHUT UP?

(*Pause.*)

EDWARD. I'm sorry. I spend too much time in front of judges. (*Pause.*) Come on. Let's be reasonable about this. If I had threatened to rape her, would she be having dinner with me?

ANDREW. I don't know anything about any dinner.

EDWARD. You just heard me on the phone with her. I admit, we had a nasty fight, but she came back to the office today, we talked it out, and she went back to work. Now I'm taking her to dinner to smooth things over.

ANDREW. A dinner is supposed to smooth over rape?

EDWARD. I did not in fact rape her! Can we at least agree on that?

ANDREW. Fine.

EDWARD. Thank you. Now. May I take it that you object to this dinner?

ANDREW. Yes. I object to the dinner.

EDWARD. Why?

ANDREW. Edward—

EDWARD. Are you interested in her?

ANDREW. You know—she is not some thing we can pass around between us, Jesus—

EDWARD. You're objecting to a simple dinner. I'm trying to find out why. If there's something going on between you—

ANDREW. No, nothing is going on between us!

EDWARD. You don't want her, but you'd prefer that no one else had her?

ANDREW. I don't know what it is about you, but everything sounds so sleazy coming out of your mouth.

EDWARD. Yeah, they teach us how to do that in law school. I'm just trying to get a grip on this, man. I mean, it sounds to me like you want to fuck her.

ANDREW. Everything is not sex, you know?

EDWARD. I know. Do you want to fuck her or not?

ANDREW. Look, I'm engaged to another woman, I'm not about to—why am I even answering you? I'm not the one on trial here!

EDWARD. Oh, no. Not Lydia. I have told you, I absolutely refuse to believe that you are going to marry that woman—

ANDREW. We are not getting into this again—

EDWARD. Sleeping with Lydia is one thing, Andrew, but marrying her—·

ANDREW. We are not discussing this—

EDWARD. Come on, the woman looks like a corpse! What happens when you dust her off and actually put her in sunlight?

ANDREW. You didn't object to her looks while you were going out with her! As I recall, before she dumped you, you thought she was "exquisite."

EDWARD. Ooooo. Nice shot. That's a three pointer. (*HE exits to the kitchen and returns a moment later with fixings for hors d' oeurves. HE eats happily.*)

ANDREW. (*Pause.*) I don't know why I even talk to you anymore.

EDWARD. (*Calling.*) I keep you sharp.

ANDREW. (*Calling.*) You give me a headache.

EDWARD. (*Reentering.*) I love fighting with you. You're so earnest.

ANDREW. Oh, for—yes, I'm earnest. Jesus CHRIST, I'm earnest! This is not a game—

EDWARD. ANDREW. CALM DOWN. I know it's not a game. I'm just being a jerk, okay?

ANDREW. Well, cut it out. I mean, some things are not just food for another argument. We're talking about a woman's soul here—

EDWARD. A woman's soul? Andrew, come back. We're not talking about anybody's *soul*; we're talking about whether or not I said something sleazy to my secretary. I'm not trying to be difficult; I'm just being realistic. I mean, I just, I don't want to have a little conversation about how we all should behave better so the world will be a better place. I'm not going to make the world a better place. The human race does not do that. We make it worse, we always have; if we're not killing each other, we're killing whales or buffalo or bald eagles, what have you, and if we're not doing that, we just pollute everything so nothing can survive here anyway. That is what the human race does; it's what we've always done. We have our moments. We have Shakespeare. The Declaration of Independence. The Taj Mahal. Smokey Robinson. We are capable of wisdom and compassion and genius, but most of the time we just throw it away. We yearn for meaning and then we squander our lives on drugs and television. We're corrupt. We are not good. I accept that. And this is why you're holed up in this nice little university teaching political philosophy, and I'm making $143,000 a year defending drug dealers. Because I like reality. And what is the moral of this story? The moral is: Georgie is real. She is *real*. And frankly, your impulse to keep her at a distance, physically, at least, strikes me as a little academic.

ANDREW. Don't give me that. What are you saying, I'm stupid or insipid because I want to preserve some integrity in my private life, because I believe it's possible to—to—to care about her without screwing her? I believe in human dignity so I'm an idiot, is that it? Well, fuck you, Edward. I mean it. That's a crock of shit. Next thing, you'll be telling me Ted Bundy is a national hero!

EDWARD. Don't twist my words. My position is offensive enough as it stands. Chill out. Have some scotch. (*HE pours him a drink.*) Come on. We can talk about this. We've been through worse.

ANDREW. I don't know. I don't know. Sometimes, talking to you is like talking to a swamp.

EDWARD. It's a gift.

ANDREW. I have to admit, it is.

(*THEY drink.*)

EDWARD. This is good scotch. When did you start drinking scotch?

ANDREW. Last night.

EDWARD. Oh?

ANDREW. Yeah. We had a fight of our own. She blames me for the whole thing. As far as she's concerned, I gave you permission to threaten rape.

EDWARD. Well—in a way—

ANDREW. Edward—

EDWARD. Sorry. I'm sorry. It's like a knee jerk reaction. I'm sorry.

ANDREW. Look. I admit this is largely my fault. I never should have sent her to you in the first place. I wasn't thinking. I thought you'd treat her differently because she came from me.

EDWARD. Andrew.

ANDREW. I know. That was pretty stupid, wasn't it? I am a stupid man.

EDWARD. Andrew—I'm sorry. I am sorry. I just don't know what I can do about it now. You want me to promise to behave myself? I can promise that.

ANDREW. Please don't take this wrong, but I would have to be crazy to trust your promises at this point. God only knows what the word "behave" actually means to you.

EDWARD. It has a series of definitions.

ANDREW. Exactly. I'll get her another job.

EDWARD. What?

ANDREW. Don't give me a hard time about this! If she goes back to work for you, it's like she's saying fine, treat me like dirt, I don't mind. Well, she's better than that, all right?

EDWARD. It's not like she's Joan of Arc, for God's sake.

ANDREW. I'm not going to argue about this anymore.

EDWARD. It just seems to me that complete relocation is a drastic solution to an essentially simple misunderstanding. I don't think it's necessary, okay?

ANDREW. Well, I think it is.

(Pause.)

EDWARD. Well, what you think isn't entirely relevant anymore, is it?

ANDREW. (Pause.) Excuse me?

EDWARD. (Dangerous.) Look. I spent the last four months training that girl and she is now a damn good secretary. I'm not going to let you just walk off with her.

ANDREW. Oh, now everything's business all of a sudden—

EDWARD. What else would it be?

ANDREW. Was it business when you threatened to rape her? And this dinner, that's business too, huh?

(Pause.)

EDWARD. You know, you're getting to be a real prick in your old age.

ANDREW. That's funny, coming from you.

(Pause.)

EDWARD. So what are you going to do? You going to tell her that she can't work for me anymore? You're going to tell her that, huh?

ANDREW. I'm just going to talk to her. She'll quit.

EDWARD. She isn't going to quit! She doesn't give a fuck about your moral codes, Andrew! She needs the damn job.

ANDREW. I'm just going to talk to her.

EDWARD. Tell you what. We'll both talk to her. When she gets down here, we'll just ask her. The two of us. We'll just ask her if she wants to quit.

ANDREW. I would prefer to talk to her alone.

EDWARD. Uh huh. I just bet you would.

ANDREW. Listen—

EDWARD. No, I understand. You two need a little privacy to work out the details of this decent little friendship you got.

ANDREW. It's not—

(KNOCKS on door.)

EDWARD. How much time do you need?

ANDREW. I don't—

EDWARD. It took me five minutes to get her to come back. How much time do you need to get her to quit again?

GEORGIE. *(KNOCKING.)* Hey, are you guys in there?

EDWARD. Ten minutes. Will that do?

ANDREW. You know—Lydia really is right about you.

EDWARD. I'll give you fifteen. That's ten more than I had. And I'll bet you, you still can't do it. How about it, Andrew?

ANDREW. I am not going to bet you—

GEORGIE. *(POUNDING.)* You guys—

EDWARD. You're on. Come up with some sort of excuse, okay? Hello, my darling.

(EDWARD opens the door. GEORGIE enters; SHE is dressed to the nines in a provocative outfit. In her hands, SHE carries a pair of exotic spike heels.)

GEORGIE. Hi, Eddie. Have a little trouble with the door there? (*SHE crosses and puts on her shoes.*)

EDWARD. You're late.

GEORGIE. So fire me. The subway went insane yet again. It took me forever to get home. Hi, Andrew.

EDWARD. You should have said something. I could have given you a lift.

GEORGIE. No, it's okay, I love the subway.

(*SHE puts on the second shoe and stands up a little too quickly. SHE staggers; EDWARD reaches out and steadies her.*)

EDWARD. Steady—

GEORGIE. Sorry. I haven't worn these things for a while and you have to get used to them, you know? It's kind of like walking on stilts.

EDWARD. They're fabulous. You really look stunning, Georgie.

GEORGIE. I'm not overdressed, am I?

EDWARD. No, no. I mean, you don't have to be. (*Pause.*) That's not what I mean. I mean, we can go someplace elegant. If—we go out, I mean.

GEORGIE. What do you mean, if?

EDWARD. Nothing.

GEORGIE. Great. Let's go. (*SHE turns for the door.*)

EDWARD. Andrew?

GEORGIE. Andrew. Well, what a fun idea. Andrew. Why don't you come along?

ANDREW. I don't think—

GEORGIE. If you're not hungry, you can always watch us eat.

(Pause.)

ANDREW. No. Thank you.

GEORGIE. Suit yourself. *(To Edward.)* Andrew's in a snit, huh? He doesn't like it when I wear these shoes. He thinks they're bad for me. But you like them, don't you?

EDWARD. I have to admit, I do. Sorry, Andrew.

GEORGIE. I like them, too. I like the way they make my legs look kind of dangerous. And I like being tall. *(SHE laughs.)* I like being able to look you both in the eye. It's the only chance I get, when I'm wearing these things. *(SHE crosses to Edward and stands close, looking him in the eye.)* See what I mean?

EDWARD. It's perfectly delightful.

GEORGIE. Thank you. *(SHE looks back at Andrew.)* What do you think, Andrew?

ANDREW. I think they look sad and ridiculous.

GEORGIE. Then I guess it's a good thing you're not going out to dinner with us, huh? Come on, Edward. Let's hit the road.

ANDREW. What's your rush?

(Pause.)

GEORGIE. Excuse me?

ANDREW. You don't have to rush off, do you? Why don't you guys stay and have a drink first?

GEORGIE. I think we're in kind of a hurry.

ANDREW. One drink.

GEORGIE. Aren't we in a hurry?

ANDREW. Are you? Edward?

EDWARD. I don't think so.

ANDREW. Maybe you could run downstairs and get a bottle of wine.

EDWARD. Well, there's an idea. I'll be right back.

GEORGIE. No, Edward—I mean, I don't like wine. Look, Andrew has this scotch here. So Andrew, you've taken up scotch, huh? Forget the wine. I'll have scotch.

ANDREW. I'd really like some wine.

GEORGIE. What are you talking about? You're drinking scotch.

ANDREW. I'd rather have wine.

GEORGIE. Well, fine, then you go get it.

EDWARD. No, that's okay, I'll get it. What would you like?

ANDREW. I don't—Champagne.

GEORGIE. What?

ANDREW. We'll have champagne. It'll be fun.

GEORGIE. Fun?

EDWARD. I'll be right back.

GEORGIE. No, come on—I mean—okay. I'll go get it.

ANDREW and EDWARD. (*Overlapping.*) NO. No, no—

(*GEORGIE stares at them.*)

EDWARD. I mean—it'll just take a second. You two—can chat.

GEORGIE. I don't want to chat.

EDWARD. Chat.

(HE exits. GEORGIE turns and stares at Andrew for a second, then crosses and pours herself a glass of scotch.)

GEORGIE. Okay. What is going on?

ANDREW. I might ask you the same question.

GEORGIE. Hey, I'm not the one acting like the three stooges, okay?

ANDREW. What do you think you're doing?

GEORGIE. What do I think I'm doing? I think I'm giving Edward a hard-on. What do you think I'm doing?

ANDREW. I don't know. *(Pause.)* Are you trying to make me jealous?

GEORGIE. Is it working?

ANDREW. Yeah. Sure.

GEORGIE. Good.

ANDREW. I can't believe you. You went back to work for him. After what he did, you went back to work—you're going out to *dinner—*

GEORGIE. You're suggesting we all have champagne together. So get off my fucking back, okay? It looks like we're two of a kind when it comes to Edward.

ANDREW. I was trying to get rid of him so I could talk to you for a few minutes!

GEORGIE. Really? Andrew, you're so sly.

ANDREW. Okay, fine. You're mad at me, you want to have a fight, fine—

GEORGIE. Gee, thanks for the permission, teach—

ANDREW. But don't go back to work for him! Don't have dinner with him!

GEORGIE. Why not?

ANDREW. He threatened to rape you!

GEORGIE. He apologized!

ANDREW. I would like to think that some things go beyond apology.

GEORGIE. Like what? Like betrayal, maybe? Listen—I know he's still slime, but you want to know what happened? I did go back to work, yeah. I went back in to get my stuff—I had all this shit in my desk, you know? So I go in at about ten to pick it all up, and it was amazing. Every secretary in the building has her own little story to tell me about how she almost did the same thing but never had the guts. I'm like this fucking hero, you know? So right in the middle of this big scene, there's like fifteen people crowding around my desk, right, Edward comes out and says he wants to talk to me. In his office. And he just stands there, and it's like this dare, you know, it's like this fucking dare, and everyone goes real quiet, just waiting to see what I'm gonna do. The whole fucking office is watching me. So we go in, and he apologizes. Swore he'd never do it again. Then he offers me a two thousand dollar raise. Well—the whole thing just started to seem kind of funny. Two thousand bucks? He never even touched me! I didn't even have to kiss him. I just thought—hey, you know, two thousand bucks. Jesus. So—I didn't quit. (*Pause.*) I didn't quit.

ANDREW. Do you believe him?

GEORGIE. Yeah. I believe he's going to give me a raise. He won't even feel it. Two thousand is like what he pays to have his car waxed.

ANDREW. That's not what I mean.

GEORGIE. I know.

(*Pause.*)

ANDREW. I can get you another job. Last night I called some people in the department and I found some leads—

GEORGIE. I don't need a job. I got a job.

ANDREW. You don't have to put up with it. He'll try it again, you know he will—

GEORGIE. I can take care of myself; I been doing it for years. I don't need you to like, worry about me.

ANDREW. I beg to differ.

GEORGIE. Yeah, well, tough shit for you.

ANDREW. (*Pause.*) This isn't about the job.

GEORGIE. I'm getting out of here; you make me crazy—(*SHE goes for the door.*)

ANDREW. Last night you said you were in love with me.

GEORGIE. Yeah. I remember

(Pause.)

ANDREW. Come here, Please? I can't talk to you if you keep trying to leave. Come on, sit down—

(HE crosses to her at the door. Instinctively, her arms fly up, defensive.)

GEORGIE. Andrew, don't—(*Pause.*) I just—could you not get too close to me?

(Wounded, ANDREW backs off. SHE stands at the door and looks at him.)

ANDREW. I'm sorry about what happened. I didn't mean to betray you, and I certainly never meant to hurt you, and if that's why you're doing this—

GEORGIE. What exactly am I doing? (*Pause.*) You don't know, do you? You don't know if I'm just trying to make you jealous, or if this is just what is, you know, reality, why not sleep with him? Maybe this is me. Okay? I mean, I understand this. Hormones I get. Every man I've every had to deal with—I fucking know how to deal with that, okay? I know what to do, and when to do it, and how to get what I want. You know—I live in a whole different world from you. I'm in the receiver's position. I do what you guys tell me to; I always do it. Whether it's reading books or fucking, I do it. I make all this noise, you know; I scream and yell bloody fucking murder but I always manage to do what you say. That's the way we survive. I'm just being realistic, okay? And yeah, maybe I am trying to make you jealous, maybe I want to teach you something for a change, you could learn from me, but— fuck. Jesus. Forget it. (*SHE crosses from him and sits.*)

ANDREW. You're not that. You're not.

GEORGIE. Yeah, well then you tell me what I am because I don't know anymore. Oh, fuck. Look—I'm sorry I'm being so awful, I don't—I'm just confused, okay? I don't want to talk about this. Fuck. I don't know what I'm doing, Andrew, I just don't know what else to—

ANDREW. It's okay. It's okay. (*ANDREW crosses to her, tentative.*) Let me take those off. Please? Let me take your shoes off.

(SHE looks at him, amazed, as HE kneels and takes her shoes off, setting them aside. HE holds her feet between his hands for a moment.)

GEORGIE. Andrew, don't. Come on. Don't. It's killing me, okay? I know it's nothing to you, but I can't take it.
ANDREW. (*Looks at her.*) It's not nothing.

(HE holds her by the elbow and slowly leans in to kiss her. The kiss begins to become passionate and physical when HE suddenly pulls away. Confused, SHE clings to him for a moment; HE gently releases himself.)

ANDREW. (*Pause.*) Oh, God. You scare me to death.
GEORGIE. What?
ANDREW. You—no. No.
GEORGIE. Wait a minute. Come on. Let's go back to this tender moment thing—

(SHE reaches for him; HE pulls away.)

ANDREW. Look at that dress.
GEORGIE. What?
ANDREW. You look ridiculous.
GEORGIE. You just said—could you not fuck with my brain here? I get enough of that at the office—
ANDREW. Why are you wearing those shoes?
GEORGIE. Because they make my legs look good! Why are you yelling at me?
ANDREW. Because you're making a spectacle of yourself.

GEORGIE. Listen, the popular opinion is that I clean up pretty good, so don't get started on me here—

ANDREW. You don't care, do you? You're just going to go ahead and squander yourself. This is enough for you? The shoes, the dress, the fancy dinner. That's what you want, is that it?

GEORGIE. No. No, I don't want him, I don't want to do this, if you don't want me to, I won't do it—I—Why are you yelling at me? A minute ago you were kissing me, and you meant it. You meant it. Why are you yelling at me? What the FUCK is going on here?

ANDREW. (*Pause.*) It wouldn't work. We are too different. There is an abyss between us; not a crevice, not a difference of opinion. An abyss. The void. It would be a nightmare to negotiate, and you're not exactly the calmest person I've ever met, you know what I mean? Who do you think you'd take it out on?

GEORGIE. I wouldn't.

ANDREW. Who are you kidding? It's inevitable with you; there's no peace in you. The only reason we've lasted as long as we have is because we don't sleep together. I listen to you, and I feel battered. I wouldn't survive. I'm telling you, if it got to be any more than this, I would not survive. (*Pause.*) It doesn't have to be like this. Life doesn't have to be just this long scream of rage, Georgie. You're better than this. I made you better than this.

GEORGIE. What?

ANDREW. I'm sorry. I didn't mean that.

GEORGIE. What did you say? You made me better? Did you actually say that?

ANDREW. Please don't go off again, I cannot take any more of this—

GEORGIE. (*Picks up the shoes.*) Well, I won't be better. I won't be better anymore. I'll be as bad as I want. Why didn't you just leave me alone in the first place; why didn't you just let me be whatever I was? At least I was happy. (*SHE starts to put on the shoes again.*)

ANDREW. You weren't happy.

GEORGIE. Fuck you. I'm not happy now.

ANDREW. You were not happy. You were so bored with your life you were killing yourself. You came home drunk after every shift; you were sleeping with every guy who looked at you—

GEORGIE. That's what this is all about, isn't it? Fuck the abyss, this isn't about any abyss, this is about sex! All the guys. That's what bothers you, really. Isn't it?

ANDREW. Oh, for God's sake, I'm not judging you. Your apartment's right above mine. I couldn't help—the whole building knew about it. Christ.

GEORGIE. Why don't you just cut my heart out and get it over with? Compared to you, Edward really is a prince. Tell him I went upstairs to wait.

ANDREW. Georgie—

GEORGIE. TELL HIM I'M WAITING FOR HIM UPSTAIRS.

ANDREW. It won't prove anything.

GEORGIE. Oh, yeah. It will. Think about it, Andrew. Think about it tonight, while you're listening to your little ceiling here. Think about it.

(*SHE exits. ANDREW stands for a moment, then viciously shoves a pile of books off the bookcase.*)

BLACKOUT

ACT II

Scene 1

Loud MUSIC is heard on the boombox, Elvis Costello or Prince. The LIGHTS come up on Georgie's apartment, layout identical to that in Andrew's apartment, but all particulars—knickknacks, books, pillows, etc., different. This apartment is a comfortable mess. Georgie actually has more books than Andrew; they sprawl everywhere, as do her tapes.

EDWARD and GEORGIE are discovered entwined in a serious clinch on the couch. GEORGIE's legs are wrapped around Edward's body, the spike heels clearly visible. After a moment, EDWARD suddenly pulls away. HE looks down at Georgie for a moment, stands, crosses to the MUSIC and snaps it off. GEORGIE watches him, astonished. HE remains standing by the silent boombox for a moment before she speaks.

GEORGIE. Is something wrong?

EDWARD. The music. It seemed a little loud to me.

GEORGIE. Oh. (*Pause.*) Well, then, why don't you turn it off?

EDWARD. Thanks, I think I will.

(Pause. HE stands there, thinking. SHE looks at him.)

GEORGIE. Edward—

53

EDWARD. Could I have something to drink?

GEORGIE. Excuse me?

EDWARD. You invited me up for a drink. I'd like a drink.

GEORGIE. I'm sorry. I'm a little confused. I thought we got *past* the drink.

EDWARD. I'm kind of thirsty.

(Pause.)

GEORGIE. Okay. What would you like to drink?

EDWARD. I don't know, I—tea? Could I have a cup of tea?

GEORGIE. Excuse me?

EDWARD. I think I'd like some tea.

GEORGIE. Why?

EDWARD. Don't you have any tea?

GEORGIE. I don't know, you know, I kind of doubt it—

EDWARD. I'll look.

GEORGIE. Edward—

(HE exits to the kitchen. NOISE. GEORGIE looks after him, annoyed, then sits and stares at the coffee table for a moment. SHE suddenly picks up a pile of books and drops them on the floor, crosses to the table, pours herself a drink.)

GEORGIE. (*Calling loudly.*) I think you're going to have to settle for scotch, Edward. Personally, I have always thought scotch was much more to the point than almost \[anly\]thing else available in most situations.

EDWARD. (*Calling.*) I'd like to keep my wits about me, if you don't mind.

GEORGIE. (*Drinking.*) Oh, you plan on needing your wits? What for?

EDWARD. (*Reentering.*) One never knows. You know, your kitchen is a disaster area. And how old is this stuff? (*HE carries a mashed box of tea.*)

GEORGIE. I have no idea.

EDWARD. That milk in there, you know, that stuff is really frightening. (*HE goes back into the kitchen.*)

GEORGIE. (*Calling.*) Edward—

EDWARD. (*Calling, SOUND OF DISHES.*) Don't you ever wash your dishes? Andrew's always complaining about the bugs in this building; I don't see how you can just leave dirty plates lying around like this. It's like an invitation

GEORGIE. Edward—EDWARD. You are not doing my dishes. YOU ARE NOT—

(*SHE stands and crosses quickly.
EDWARD meets her in the doorway.*)

EDWARD. SHHHH. Could—would you be quiet, please? You are one of the noisiest people I've ever met. It's the middle of the night, people are trying to sleep.

GEORGIE. Not everyone. Some of them, I'm sure, are doing other things. People do all sorts of things in the middle of the night. Didn't you know that?

EDWARD. Yes. I know that.

GEORGIE. I thought maybe you did. So—what's the problem here, Edward? All of a sudden you're acting like—I mean, what, is this your first time?

EDWARD. No.

GEORGIE. You a little nervous? You want me to be gentle? I can be gentle. (*SHE starts to close in.*)

EDWARD. That's not necessary.

GEORGIE. I didn't think it was. So what's the problem?

EDWARD. I'm just trying to get a grip on this. I mean, not two days ago, you did tell me, and I quote, "Even if you were the last fucking asshole on the planet, Edward—"

GEORGIE. Yeah, yeah, yeah. What can I say? I came to my senses.

EDWARD. Yes, well—

GEORGIE. You can be very persuasive.

EDWARD. I'm aware of that; still—

GEORGIE. You changing your mind about this?

EDWARD. No, that's not exactly—

GEORGIE. So what's the problem? (*SHE's getting close.*)

EDWARD. There's no problem. I just—I want that tea.

(*HE goes back to the kitchen. GEORGIE looks after him, seriously annoyed.*)

GEORGIE. I swear, sex was never this complicated in high school. (*SHE looks at the floor. To floor.*) You getting all this?

(*SHE glances back at the kitchen for a moment, then stomps on the floor several times. EDWARD enters with a mug of tea and watches her.*)

EDWARD. Is something wrong?

GEORGIE. (*Starts.*) Oh. You know. Bugs. (*SHE takes off her shoe, crosses to the trash can and scrapes the bug off, puts the shoe back on.*) Got your tea there? Mmm, that looks delicious.

EDWARD. Could you turn down the sarcasm for just a few minutes, please? I mean, I would just like a minute, a tiny oasis of time that is not smothered in attitude. Just a moment of normal conversation. If you don't mind. I would like to talk.

GEORGIE. We talked at dinner.

EDWARD. No, we chatted at dinner. We had three hours of chat, and I'm feeling a little disoriented, and I would like to talk.

GEORGIE. Why?

EDWARD. What's the matter, don't you know *how* to talk?

GEORGIE. Of course I know how to talk. I talk constantly! I just don't want to talk now! Christ, you're as bad as Andrew!

EDWARD. Oh? How so?

GEORGIE. (*Pause.*) I don't want to talk about Andrew.

EDWARD. Why not?

GEORGIE. Edward—

EDWARD. What?

GEORGIE. You are driving me crazy.

EDWARD. Why are you getting so defensive?

GEORGIE. I'm not—I hate this.

EDWARD. I just asked a simple question—

GEORGIE. You did not, you—

EDWARD. Yes, I did—

GEORGIE. You're right, this talking is really fun. I'm so glad we're *talking*. Okay. So fine. So what was the question?

EDWARD. Actually, there was no question. The subject of Andrew came up and you got all tense.

GEORGIE. Why don't you pick a subject. You want to have a discussion here? Then pick a subject and let's get on with it all right?

EDWARD. All right. (*Pause.*) What do you and Andrew talk about?

GEORGIE. (*Pause.*) We talk about many things. Books and shit. America. You name it, we talk about it. Andrew and I have a very conversational relationship.

EDWARD. Does that bother you?

GEORGIE. (*Pause.*) What is that supposed to mean?

EDWARD. Nothing. He told me you had a crush on him, so I just thought—

GEORGIE. Well, he was wrong.

EDWARD. How did you two meet, anyway?

GEORGIE. Edward, what is it, I mean am I on trial here—

EDWARD. You have something to hide?

GEORGIE. NO, I—fuck. We met at the mailboxes. We live in the same building, I mean, it's not unusual—

EDWARD. What, did he try to pick you up?

GEORGIE. I hardly think so.

EDWARD. You tried to pick him up.

GEORGIE. Is there a point to this? 'Cause I got to tell you, you're kind of wrecking the mood here; you're like doing a demolition job on my hormones.

EDWARD. I just want to know how you two met! He never told me.

GEORGIE. He gave me a book. We were standing by the mailboxes, and he handed me this book and said, here, I think you'll like this. That was it. He gave me this book.

EDWARD. He gave you a book?

GEORGIE. Yes.

EDWARD. You didn't think that was a pickup?

GEORGIE. No, I thought he was a Jehovah's Witness.

EDWARD. What?

GEORGIE. I thought he was a Jehovah's Witness! I have this ongoing relationship with those guys; I'm like, a sucker for the Jehovah's Witnesses. So when this guy gave me a book I thought it was gonna be about the end of the world or what God really thinks or something. I mean, I got like the collected edition of those things—

EDWARD. You actually buy those?

GEORGIE. Yeah—well, yeah, I—I got a whole shelf of them.

(SHE indicates. HE goes over to look at her books. HE picks one up and pages through it, amazed.)

GEORGIE. What? They just get to me, okay? I mean, those fucking moonies, or the dianetics people, you can see it in their eyes, their brains are fried; they'd just as soon kill you as anything. But the Jehovah's Witnesses are always so nerdy I believe them. What? It's not like I go to their meetings or anything. I just talk to them. I like what they say. Resurrection. Life everlasting. It just sounds nice. I mean, I don't believe this shit at all, but I just—I end up listening because it's so—I don't know. They're always so kind. (*Pause.*) You can borrow that if you want. It's okay. You might like it. Some of it's very hopeful.

EDWARD. (*Looks at her and smiles.*) Thank you.

GEORGIE. So that's why I talked to Andrew. I thought he was a Jehovah's Witness. So. You want to do it or not?

EDWARD. (*Looks at her, startled and suddenly uncomfortable The mood is seriously broken.*) Excuse me?

GEORGIE. Oh, come on, Edward. We both know why you're here.

EDWARD. (*Recovering.*) Yes, I guess we do, now. And I must say, I am stunned by your subtlety. I mean— never mind. Never mind. I think I will have that drink after all. The tea is not actually doing the trick. (*HE picks the scotch bottle off the bookshelf, crosses to the kitchen and finds some ice and glasses.*)

GEORGIE. Oh, for God's sake. We're drinking now? Now we're drinking? Why are we drinking?

EDWARD. We're drinking because I want to drink!

GEORGIE. Are we going to have more conversation, too?

EDWARD. We will if I want to!

GEORGIE. Yeah, well, as long as we're taking a poll here, I gotta say, I'm not particularly interested in more conversation, Edward! I mean it. If you think this is going to go on all night or something, maybe you should just leave.

EDWARD. You're not throwing me out. (*HE reenters, pours scotch into her glass and hands it to her.*)

GEORGIE. You say one more word, and I am.

EDWARD. No, you're not.

GEORGIE. Yes, I am.

EDWARD. Drink your scotch.

GEORGIE. Fuck you.

EDWARD. Yeah, fuck you too.

(THEY bump glasses in a forced toast. THEY both drink.)

GEORGIE. Now what? Should we have another? Maybe we should go out to dinner again. No, I know. How about a game of cards?

EDWARD. You know, I have to say, you really—your technique just leaves me breathless. Really.

GEORGIE. I gave you technique all night, Edward, and it didn't get either of us anywhere. But the gig is up. I don't know what's bugging you but it's time to get over it. You want to do it or not? This is your last shot.

EDWARD. *(Pause.)* My last shot?

GEORGIE. Yeah. This is it. This is the offer. So what's it going to be?

EDWARD. Well. Since you put it that way.

(HE sets his drink down and looks at her. HE does not move. After a moment, SHE crosses slowly, eases into him and almost kisses him. HE speaks.)

EDWARD. Thank you very much, but since you put it that way, I'm afraid I'm going to have to decline your generous offer.

GEORGIE. *(Pause.)* Suit yourself. *(SHE crosses away from him, furious, and picks up her drink.)*

EDWARD. Please don't take this wrong. I just don't like being used.

GEORGIE. Oh, cut me a break. You want it; I'm saying here it is. Who cares about being used at a time like this?

EDWARD. I do.

GEORGIE. Yeah, I guess you can dish it out but you can't take it. Well, fine. That's fine. But trust me on this one: You just passed up the most interesting fuck of your life.

EDWARD. That may be. But it also may be that I prefer sleeping with one person at a time. Maybe I simply want to preserve as one of the ground rules of the increasingly neurotic relationship we seem to have established between us that if I ever do take you to bed, it will be on the condition that Andrew does not come along! (*HE puts on his jacket and starts to leave.*)

GEORGIE. Andrew—fuck Andrew, I am tired of talking about Andrew!

EDWARD. What happened, he broke your heart so now you're bitter? You poor thing.

GEORGIE. Oh, shut up—

EDWARD. And now you're going to seduce his best friend to get back at him, is that it? That's the oldest trick in the book!

GEORGIE. Yeah, it's so old you almost fell for it.

EDWARD. What do you think you're doing? You think this is going to prove something? All it proves is what I suspected from the start: You are nothing but bad news.

GEORGIE. Look who's talking.

EDWARD. I am. And I know you. I know exactly who you are.

GEORGIE. You don't know the first thing about me.

EDWARD. I know everything about you. I see you every fucking day down at the courthouse, hanging all over your junkie boyfriend, screaming at your pimp!

GEORGIE. I don't know what you're talking about.

EDWARD. *(Overlap.)* I know where you grew up. I know your family. I know how your mother lays around the house all day because she can't hold down a job—

GEORGIE. This doesn't have anything to do with anything—

EDWARD. I know how she drinks! I know how she leeches money out of you! I know about all of it, the arrests—

GEORGIE. STOP IT. *(Pause.)* So what? So you listen in on my phone calls, so what is that supposed to prove?

EDWARD. I don't listen to your phone calls. I don't have to. You're a dime a dozen, Georgie; you are as common as dirt.

GEORGIE. Yeah, I'm so common you've been trying to screw me for four months.

EDWARD. You think that makes you something? That doesn't make you anything. This is all—this is a fucking game to guys like me; you're a piece of furniture, for God's sake! I could go through three of you in a week!

GEORGIE. *(Overlap.)* Shut up. SHUT UP.

EDWARD. Come to think of it, I will take you up on that offer. Why the hell not?

GEORGIE. SHUT UP. You SHUT UP

(SHE takes a swing at him. EDWARD grabs her arms; THEY struggle for a second.)

EDWARD. Christ—Georgie, for God's sake—

GEORGIE. Shut UP! Why don't you ever SHUT UP—
(SHE stops suddenly.)

EDWARD. Georgie—

GEORGIE. Oh, shit, I can't see anything. Edward—

EDWARD. Oh, Christ—Here, put your head down—you're okay—(*HE sets her on the couch and tries to put her head down.*)

GEORGIE. No, I need air—(*Scared.*) I can't see, Edward—

EDWARD. (*Starting to panic.*) You're okay. You're fine. Just shut your eyes for a second. Take a breath. Georgie?

GEORGIE. I can't see.

(*SHE leans back on the couch. HE puts his arm around her.*)

EDWARD. You're okay. You're okay. Are you okay? Come on. Sweetheart. Are you okay?

GEORGIE. (*SHE suddenly shoves him away.*) *Don't you touch me.*

(*HE backs away, startled. Pause.*)

GEORGIE. Just stay away from me, okay?

EDWARD. Yeah. Yeah. I'm sorry. I'm sorry, okay? I'm sorry. Christ. What am I doing?

(*HE sits. Pause. SHE watches him. HE finally looks at her.*)

EDWARD. Are you okay?
GEORGIE. Yeah.
EDWARD. I'm sorry. I don't know why I did that.
GEORGIE. Me neither.
EDWARD. Can you see me?

GEORGIE. Yeah. I can see you. It just went funny, you know? When you just see stars? It went funny. I couldn't see anything. It scared me.

EDWARD. Me too.

(SHE sits up. HE starts for her, then stops.)

EDWARD. Come on. Just lie there for a second, would you?

GEORGIE. I'm okay.

EDWARD. You're not okay. You're drunk.

GEORGIE. No, I'm not. I didn't drink hardly anything. I just—I got—so mad at you. That never happened to me before. I mean, I'm, like, mad all the time, but that never happened before.

EDWARD. You just never had me around to provoke you. And that was nothing. Stick with me, baby. I'll *really* piss you off.

GEORGIE. It's not funny.

EDWARD. I know.

GEORGIE. You were being a big jerk.

EDWARD. I know. I'm sorry.

GEORGIE. Why did you do that?

EDWARD. (*Starts to cross again, and stops himself uncertainly.*) Don't think about it for a minute.

GEORGIE. Man. I have to stop getting so mad all the time.

EDWARD. You scared me half to death. Do you want a glass of water?

GEORGIE. What is this thing you have with liquids? Andrew's the same way; something goes wrong and he just dives for the liquids. I don't know, they teach you this in college? Is this a class thing?

EDWARD. I'll get you a glass of water.

(HE goes into the kitchen. GEORGIE curls up on the couch. HE returns a moment later with a glass of water and a washcloth. HE approaches her carefully, then feeds her the water as if she were a child. SHE resists for a moment.)

EDWARD. Come on, sweetheart. Just drink it. It's good for you.

GEORGIE. It's just water, Edward.

EDWARD. Water is very good for you—there you go. Here. Come on.

(SHE drinks. HE takes the cloth and wipes her face.)

EDWARD. Is that better?

GEORGIE. Yeah.

EDWARD. Good.

GEORGIE. Why are you being so nice all of a sudden?

EDWARD. Look, I am a nice person. *(SHE laughs.)* I am! Ten percent of the time, I am a very nice person. *(HE pats her face with the cloth again, then folds it neatly.)* You okay now?

GEORGIE. Yeah. Hey, Edward.

EDWARD. Yeah.

GEORGIE. What's she like? Lydia, I mean.

EDWARD. I'm not the person to ask. I don't like her.

GEORGIE. What, are you kidding? That makes you exactly the person to ask.

EDWARD. Lots of money, ancestors on the Mayflower, parents on Beacon Hill. That sort of thing.

GEORGIE. Yeah, yeah, yeah. Cut to the chase. What does she look like?

EDWARD. She's very pale. She's pretty, but pale and orderly. Quiet. I find her kind of sinister, to tell you the truth.

GEORGIE. You make her sound like Dracula.

EDWARD. Yes, she's very much like Dracula. Always meticulously dressed. You know, neat little dresses. Blouses with bows at the collar. Protruding bicuspids. (*HE bares his teeth. SHE laughs, then starts to cry.*) Hey, hey, hey.

GEORGIE. Oh, perfect. He's gonna marry Dracula; that's just perfect. I'm sorry, I'm just—

EDWARD. Hey. It's okay.

GEORGIE. It's not okay. How can he do it?

EDWARD. It's what he thinks he wants.

GEORGIE. Well, why isn't it me?

EDWARD. I don't know. He's stupid.

GEORGIE. Don't talk down to me, Edward; I don't need you to act like I'm some sort of big baby here—

EDWARD. I'm not! I mean it. He's being really stupid.

GEORGIE. Yeah, right. (*Pause. SHE dries her eyes.*)

EDWARD. Look. I'm sorry I said those things, okay? I mean, those things I said before.

GEORGIE. No, it's okay. Some of it was true.

EDWARD. Still.

GEORGIE. Yeah. Hey, Edward.

EDWARD. Yeah?

GEORGIE. Can you put your arm around me for a second?

EDWARD. Georgie—

GEORGIE. Come on. I wouldn't ask except you've been nice for about two minutes or something and I'm afraid if I wait any longer, you'll, like, turn into yourself again.

EDWARD. You're not still doing this to get back at him?

GEORGIE. For heaven's sake. It's just a hug.

(HE brushes her hair back from her face, and puts his arm around her. SHE hangs onto him for a moment, then pulls away a little. THEY sit, for a moment, with their arms around each other. SHE puts her head on his shoulder.)

GEORGIE. This is nice.

(POUNDING on the door. GEORGIE jumps then clings to Edward for a second.)

EDWARD. Well. I wonder who that is.

GEORGIE. Oh, God. I can't handle this anymore.

EDWARD. Chin up. You can't give up now, sweetheart.

(The KNOCKING becomes violent.)

GEORGIE. Edward—

EDWARD. You're fine. If he gets out of line, just throw a pencil at him.

(HE opens the door. LYDIA is there.)

EDWARD. Oh, no.

LYDIA. (*Biting.*) Hello, Edward. How lovely to see you again. (*SHE crosses into the apartment and glares at Georgie.*)

EDWARD. Lydia. What a charming coincidence. We were just talking about you.

LYDIA. That is charming.

EDWARD. Where's Andrew?

LYDIA. Who cares?

EDWARD. Oh, I think several of us, at least ... (*HE looks out in the hallway but Andrew is nowhere in sight.*)

LYDIA. How about you? Do you care?

GEORGIE. Well, I don't—

LYDIA Oh, please. I have a little trouble believing that!

GEORGIE. Listen. I don't know who you are or what you think you're doing here, but—

LYDIA. Oh, I think you know who I am.

GEORGIE. Well, of course I know who you are! What are you doing here?

LYDIA. No. What are you doing here?

GEORGIE. I live here!

LYDIA. You know what I mean!

EDWARD. Excuse me, but where's Andrew?

LYDIA. Oh, where do you think he is? He's downstairs, shrouded in the shattered wreckage of his book, our marriage and my life.

EDWARD. Oh, Christ. (*HE exits.*)

GEORGIE. Edward, hey! Hey, where are you going? Don't leave me here with her! Edward!

(But he is gone. GEORGIE turns and looks at LYDIA,
who is very steely indeed.)

GEORGIE. Look. It's been great meeting you, but you
know, I am having one ripper of a day, you know, so—
LYDIA. Don't talk to me about bad days.
GEORGIE. Listen—
LYDIA. No. No. You listen. (*SHE puts down her purse*
decisively, crosses to the door and shuts it.)
GEORGIE. HEY—
LYDIA. I don't know you. You and I have never met.
And you are wreaking havoc on my life.

(LYDIA crosses back to her purse, reaches in and pulls out
Georgie's jacket, blouse, slip, skirt, pantyhose and
shoes from the previous day. SHE folds these items and
stacks them neatly as she speaks. GEORGIE watches,
amazed.)

LYDIA. At first, I admired Andrew's interest in your
welfare. He cares about people; he truly cares and I think
that's wonderful. But these past few months, I must admit,
I have become less interested in his interest. Not only do I
listen to him talk about you incessantly, any time I come
over to have dinner or spend the night here, I am
bombarded by you. When you come home at night, we
hear your little heels clicking on the ceiling. When you
leave in the morning, we hear your little heels. When you
go to bed we hear you brush your teeth, and talk on the
phone, and listen to the radio and on certain evenings I
could swear that we can even hear you undress. I am not
enjoying this. For the past two months, I have been under

the distinct impression that any time I spend the night here, I am actually sleeping with two people—Andrew, and yourself. In fact, when you came home with Edward tonight my first thought was, my God, the bed is already crowded enough; now we have to fit Edward in too? Now. I don't know what went on between you and Andrew.

GEORGIE. Nothing. Nothing at all.

LYDIA. Excuse me, but that clearly is not the case. And I want you out of my life! Is that understood?

GEORGIE. Where am I supposed to go?

LYDIA. I don't care! I'll find you a better apartment! It will be my pleasure!

(THEY glare at each other for a moment.)

GEORGIE. Listen, I am really sorry but I am just not up to this right now, okay? I mean, if I get mad one more time tonight I might just die from it. So, can we chill out for a minute? You want a cup of tea or something?

LYDIA. Do you have anything stronger? Scotch? Is that scotch?

GEORGIE. Yes. It is.

LYDIA. I'll have scotch.

GEORGIE. Fine. (*SHE exits to the kitchen and reenters a second later with a glass. SHE pours Lydia a shot of scotch.*) Here. You knock that back, you'll feel much better.

LYDIA. Thank you. (*SHE drinks and studies Georgie.*) That's an interesting outfit you have on.

GEORGIE. Excuse me?

LYDIA. I guess men really do like that sort of thing, don't they? You'd like to think some of them, at least one, or two, are above it, but that just doesn't seem to be the case. All of them, they're like Pavlov's dogs; you provide the right stimulus and the next thing you know, they're salivating all over you. Don't those shoes hurt?

GEORGIE. Yeah, as a matter of fact, they kind of do.

LYDIA. But I guess you don't wear them for comfort, do you? You wear them for other reasons. You wear them because they make your legs look amazing. (*SHE puts the second pair of heels on and walks around the room for a moment and picks up a large book under the table.*) And I see you're also studying law.

GEORGIE. (*Crosses and takes the book from her.*) No, I am not "studying law." I stole that from the library at work so I could figure out what the fuck was going on down there.

LYDIA. Really. How remarkable.

GEORGIE. Look—

LYDIA. Could I have another?

GEORGIE. Another?

LYDIA. Please.

(*GEORGIE takes Lydia's glass from her and pours scotch into it, looks at her, and then continues to pour an enormous amount of scotch into the glass. SHE gives it back to her. LYDIA looks at it, and knocks back a solid drink. GEORGIE stares.*)

LYDIA. God, I wish I still smoked.

GEORGIE. You used to smoke?

LYDIA. Two packs a day. It was disgusting.

GEORGIE. You know—you're very different from what I thought. It's weird, meeting you. It's just—weird.

LYDIA. Oh, really? Well, what did you think I'd be like?

GEORGIE. I don't know. I mean, you're very— forceful. I guess I thought you would be kind of formal and polite. Maybe like Dracula, or something.

LYDIA. Oh. Edward told you that; that's where you got that. He is so awful. Ever since I dumped him he's been telling everybody I'm some kind of vampire. He thinks it's witty.

GEORGIE. Wait a minute. You went out with him, too?

LYDIA. Didn't you know that?

GEORGIE. Man, what do those two do, trade off girlfriends once a year or something?

LYDIA. It's certainly starting to look that way.

GEORGIE. Wait a minute, that's not what I—

LYDIA. (*Overlap.*) Really, there's no need to explain. In fact, I would prefer not to know the details.

GEORGIE. I'm just trying to tell you—

LYDIA. And I'm trying to tell you: What I've had with both of them is substantially more real than whatever this is, and I don't want to know about it. All right? I just want it to stop. All right?

GEORGIE. Right.

LYDIA. As long as we understand each other.

GEORGIE. Oh, I understand you all right. This part, I think I got down solid.

LYDIA. Good.

GEORGIE. (*Finally angry.*) But what I don't have, you know—what I want to know is—if you're so fucking real, Lydia, then what the hell are you doing here? I mean, if you're so much better than me, then why even bother? You could just wait it out and I'll drift away like a piece of paper, like nothing, right? 'Cause that's what I am. Nothing. Right? So why the fuck are you up here, taking me apart?

LYDIA. I don't think I have to justify myself to you.

GEORGIE. Oh, yeah? Well, I think you do. All of you. What an amazing fucking snow job you all are doing on the world. And I bought it! We all buy it. My family—they're like, all of a sudden I'm Mary Tyler Moore or something. I mean, they live in hell, right, and they spend their whole lives just wishing they were somewhere else, wishing they were rich, or sober, or clean; living on a street with trees, being on some fucking TV show. And I did it. I moved to Boston, I work in a law office, I'm the big success story. And they have no idea what that means. It means I get to hang out with a bunch of lunatics. It means I get to read books that make no sense. (*SHE pushes the law book off the table.*) It means that instead of getting harassed by jerks at the local bar, now I get harassed by guys in suits. Guys with glasses. Guys who talk nice. Guys in suits. Well, you know what I have to say to all of you? Shame on you. Shame on you for thinking you're better than the rest of us. And shame on you for being mean to me. Shame on you, Lydia.

LYDIA. (*Pause.*) I'm sorry.

GEORGIE. I think you'd better go.

LYDIA. Yes. Of course. (*Pause.*) I am sorry. I just—Andrew postponed our wedding tonight, and I'm a little—my life is in a bit of a shambles, tonight, and I know that's no excuse, but I'm just not myself. Please. Forgive me. (*SHE goes to the door.*)

GEORGIE. Oh, God. Wait a minute.

LYDIA. No. You're right. I've been behaving very badly. You're right. I'm sorry. *(SHE turns and opens the door.)*

GEORGIE. No, I'm the one. Come on, I'm being a jerk. He postponed the wedding? Fuck me. I'm sorry, you said that before and it went right by me. I'm sorry. I got a bad temper, and—whatever. Just sit down, okay?

(GEORGIE brings her back into the room. LYDIA pulls away.)

LYDIA. Really, I think I'd best go. Please. Please don't be nice to me. I don't want to be friends with you.

GEORGIE. Yeah, I don't want to be friends with you either. I'm just saying. I didn't mean to, like, yell at you. I think you better finish your drink.

(SHE hands her scotch to her. LYDIA looks at it for a moment then sits and drinks.)

GEORGIE. He's probably just nervous. Weddings make boys nervous.

LYDIA. I think it's worse than that. He—we haven't had sex in quite a while.

GEORGIE. You mean *none* of us are getting laid? No wonder we're all so uptight.

LYDIA. You mean you and Edward didn't—

GEORGIE. No.

LYDIA. No?

GEORGIE. No. I swear to God, I worked on him for four hours and I couldn't get him *near* the bedroom.

LYDIA. Edward? You couldn't—Edward?

GEORGIE. You didn't have that problem, huh?

LYDIA. As a matter of fact—never mind.

GEORGIE. He wanted it.

LYDIA. Yes, dear, he always wants it. Well. If he wouldn't sleep with you, I think you must've really made an impression on him.

(THEY laugh a little.)

LYDIA. And I know you've made an impression on Andrew.

GEORGIE. (*Awkward.*) Oh. I don't know.

LYDIA. Please. Could we not—? (*Pause.*) I'd prefer not to pretend. I'd also prefer not to talk to you about it, but I just don't know who else to talk to.

GEORGIE. Hey—

LYDIA. I'm not crying! It's just, I can't talk to my family about this; they'll simply gloat. They never liked Andrew. He wasn't "good" enough. Is that unbelievable? He's the best man I've ever met, and he's not *good* enough for them. He doesn't make enough money. And they certainly don't like his politics. Edward was the one they liked. Well. You can imagine. You know what my father told me, when Andrew and I decided to get married? Never trust a man who thinks he can change the world. That's what he said! I don't care, really, I don't—but how can I tell them this? I always told him, he didn't understand, just didn't understand. Andrew saved me. He is my best self; he makes me my best self. How can I tell them they were right?

GEORGIE. They're not.

LYDIA. No, I know. They're not. I know. It's just—
I'm confused.

GEORGIE. Yeah. Me too. (*Pause.*) You want to
dance? (*SHE crosses to the boombox and puts in a tape.
Romantic MUSIC comes up.*)

LYDIA. Excuse me?

GEORGIE. Come on. Dance with me.

LYDIA. What?

GEORGIE. It'll make you feel better. I'll lead and you
can just dance—

LYDIA. Oh, no—

GEORGIE. Come on. Let me do this—(*SHE unties
Lydia's bow and takes her in her arms.*)

LYDIA. I don't—aw, no—I don't dance—

GEORGIE. No, it's not silly. It's just nice. Haven't
you ever danced with a girl before? It's nice. Come on.

*(GEORGIE takes her by the arms and THEY begin to slow
dance.)*

GEORGIE. I love to dance. It's so fucking romantic.
You know? It always makes me want to have sex. Men are
so dumb, they're so busy trying to get you in bed they
can't even figure that out. I mean—I'm not making a pass
at you.

LYDIA. I understand.

*(GEORGIE nods, and THEY begin to dance more freely,
GEORGIE leading and coaxing Lydia into the moves.
As THEY turn through the room their movements
become looser, more hilariously erotic. THEY laugh for
a moment, and end up slow dancing. Suddenly, there are*

sound of a loud STRUGGLE and POUNDING on the door.)

EDWARD. *(Off.)* Georgie! Open the door! Georgie!
GEORGIE. Oh, what now?
ANDREW. *(Off.)* LET GO OF ME!
LYDIA. Oh, no—

(Both WOMEN start for the door, then stop and stare at each other.)

GEORGIE. You know, we probably—probably we should just leave them out there.

(The STRUGGLE at the door sounds even more violent.)

EDWARD. *(Off.)* GEORGIE. OPEN THE GODDAMN DOOR!

(SHE goes to the door. LYDIA turns off the MUSIC. EDWARD bursts in, dragging Andrew by the collar and sleeve. HE throws him into the room. THEY all stare at each other.)

EDWARD. Hi, girls. How's it going?
GEORGIE. Edward, what are you doing?
EDWARD. I'm trying to keep us all out of court. Now, I think it's about time we talked this out. Andrew?
ANDREW What?
EDWARD. Start talking.
GEORGIE. Actually, I think that now is not a good time, Edward.

EDWARD. Georgie, I am not going to let him do this to you anymore.

ANDREW. Let me, excuse me, let me? Who put you in charge here?

EDWARD. Just talk to her, Andrew.

GEORGIE. I mean it, you guys. Lydia and I were doing just fine here—

LYDIA. It's all right, Georgie—

ANDREW. No, it's not all right! I resent this! Who does he think he is, shoving everybody around?

EDWARD. I'm trying to help!

ANDREW. Help? You threatened to rape her, and now you think you can—

EDWARD. Wait a minute—

LYDIA. He what?

ANDREW. He threatened to rape her—

GEORGIE. You guys.

EDWARD. That is not exactly what—

LYDIA. Edward, for God's sake—

EDWARD. We were having a fight!

LYDIA. Oh, but really—

EDWARD. COULD WE NOT GO BACK TO THIS? I'M ALREADY PAST THIS POINT. (*Pause.*) Come on, Andrew. Deal with this woman.

ANDREW. Excuse me, but I don't need you to tell me what I have to do here—

EDWARD. Look, I'm on your side—

ANDREW. You are not on my—

EDWARD. Don't fight me, Andrew—

ANDREW. I will fight you if I want! (*HE shoves him.*)

EDWARD. Don't you fucking shove me—

(HE shoves him back. GEORGIE immediately leaps in between them.)

LYDIA. ANDREW.
GEORGIE. EDWARD. *(SHE stands in between them for a moment as THEY glare at each other.)* I will not have this! *(SHE shoves them both away from each other.)* You are both driving me crazy.

(SHE storms into the kitchen. The OTHER THREE stare at each other. GEORGIE reenters a moment later with a six pack of diet Pepsi which SHE passes around silently.)

EDWARD. What am I supposed to do with this?
GEORGIE. You're supposed to drink it, Edward. We are all going to just have a drink and calm down for a minute, okay? Drink it!

(EVERYONE pops their soda—and drinks. Pause.)

GEORGIE. Okay. So—could we not fight anymore? I mean, could we just like, finish our sodas and go to bed now?
EDWARD. Actually, going to bed may just be the most complicated action we could contemplate at this moment in time.
ANDREW. Georgie, can I talk to you alone? Would two you mind if I talked to her alone for a second?
LYDIA. I'd mind.
EDWARD. Yes, I think I'd mind too.
ANDREW Oh, come on—

GEORGIE. Edward, I thought you wanted to help.

EDWARD. I do want to help, but I'm also a little mad right now, and besides which we all know what he's going to say anyway. Don't we?

LYDIA. I think we do.

EDWARD. So I think he should just say it. This involves all of us. So—just say it, Andrew.

ANDREW. Forget it.

EDWARD. No, come on. Say it.

GEORGIE. You guys—

EDWARD. You want to say it. Say it!

ANDREW. I don't want to say it.

EDWARD. Say it!

GEORGIE. Edward!

LYDIA. Please, Andrew. Just say it. (*Pause. ANDREW looks at her.*) Please. It's not like I don't already know.

ANDREW. Fine. Fine. (*To Georgie.*) You were right. I think I probably—my feelings for you are stronger—All right. I am in love with you. All right?

GEORGIE. All right.

(Pause.)

LYDIA. Well, that is just *great*. (*SHE throws her drink at him.*)

ANDREW. Lydia—

LYDIA. I can't believe you said that! In front of me!

ANDREW. You told me to!

LYDIA. You're in love with her?

ANDREW. You said you knew!

LYDIA. You mean it, don't you? You're in love with her!

ANDREW. Well, of course I mean it. What else would I mean?

LYDIA. You could mean anything! I thought you meant—I don't know what I thought you meant! You jerk! You're in love with her! I mean, I can see sleeping with her, but falling in love with her?

GEORGIE. Watch it, Lydia.

LYDIA. I'm sorry—

ANDREW. I never slept with her—

LYDIA. Oh, please—

EDWARD. He didn't!

ANDREW. I didn't!

LYDIA. Well, you should've; it might've—you're in love with her?

ANDREW. Yes. (*Pause.*) I think we'd better call the wedding off altogether.

LYDIA. Yes, that would seem to be the next step, wouldn't it? You're in love with another woman; that could potentially interfere with our wedding plans.

ANDREW. Lydia, it's not you.

LYDIA. That much is clear, Andrew, I think I'm pretty straight on that point.

ANDREW. That's not what I—it's just me, okay? Things have not been—great with us for a long time, and I'm just saying, it's not enough, you're not—(*HE stops himself.*)

LYDIA. Go on. I'm not enough what? I'm not wild enough? I'm not sexy enough? I'm not passionate, I'm not needy, I'm not—I am just what I've always been, Andrew. What is suddenly not enough?

ANDREW. We can't talk about this here—

LYDIA. What kind of a life do you think you can have with her? We have a life together, we have—Georgie, I'm sorry, I don't mean this to be as insulting as it sounds, but honestly. Do you think this is going to work out? Andrew. Do you honestly think that?

ANDREW. I don't think anything. I'm just not going to lie about it anymore. (*Pause.*) I'm sorry.

LYDIA. It doesn't matter. I can learn not to love you. You learned not to love me, I can—could you take your glasses off, please? Just take them off.

(*HE takes them off and looks at her.*)

LYDIA. There. You see? When you take them off, you look like a stranger, you look—I always think that when I see you in the morning. You look like a stranger without your glasses. Except you don't, really, I don't—

ANDREW. Lydia—

LYDIA. Could you please be quiet, please? (*Pause.*) It isn't working. Put your glasses on.

(*HE puts his glasses on. Pause. LYDIA turns to Georgie.*)

LYDIA. Well, Georgie, he's all yours. If you want him, you can have him.

GEORGIE. Thanks. Yeah, thanks a lot, Lydia. And Edward, thank you. Thank you for helping us clear all this up. We all feel much better now. And Andrew, thank you for picking me up out of the gutter and teaching me how to talk and how to behave and how to read. It was really great of you. I'm just, so glad I've met you all. I'm really just— this is working out just *great*.

(SHE walks out the door, slamming it behind them. THEY all stare at the closed door.)

LYDIA. She's right. *(SHE goes to the door, opens it, leaves. The MEN stare at the closed door.)*
EDWARD. Oh, great. They're teaming up. Now we're really in for it.

(ANDREW looks at him.)

BLACKOUT

Scene 2

The next morning. The LIGHTS come up on Georgie's apartment, in much the same condition as the night before, except for the fact that EDWARD is sprawled on the couch, sleeping, and ANDREW is sprawled on the floor, tangled in blankets and a pillow. HE turns and gets himself even more tangled up. HE has not had an easy night. HE sits up, frustrated, untangles himself from the blankets, and looks at EDWARD, who is sleeping soundly. ANDREW looks at his watch, looks at Edward, picks up his pillow, crosses to Edward, and hits him with it. EDWARD jolts awake.

EDWARD. What? What?
ANDREW. Get up.
EDWARD. Why? What time is it?

ANDREW. It's after ten.

EDWARD. Did she come back?

ANDREW. No.

EDWARD. Man. This couch is really comfortable.

ANDREW. Oh, shut up.

EDWARD. Hey, I didn't tell you to sleep on the floor. You could have gone downstairs and slept in your own bed.

ANDREW. Excuse me, but since you wouldn't leave—

EDWARD. You could've slept in her bed.

ANDREW. I didn't want to sleep in her bed. It would have been ...

EDWARD. Disappointing, under the circumstances?

ANDREW. Shut up.

EDWARD. You think she's got anything to eat around here?

(HE stands and crosses to the kitchen. ANDREW watches him, somewhat amazed.)

ANDREW. How can you think about food at a time like this?

EDWARD. *(Off.)* It's ten o'clock in the morning. It's a great time to think about food.

ANDREW. Don't you have someplace to go? Something to do? A judge to bribe? Some drug kingpin to get off on a technicality?

EDWARD. *(Reentering.)* Hey. Could you let me eat something before we get into this? Besides, it's Saturday. Courts are closed. *(HE carries with him a box of cereal, which HE pours into a bowl and starts to eat without milk.)*

ANDREW. That is just—what—how can you eat that without milk?

EDWARD. She doesn't have any milk. I mean, she has some, but it's alive. You don't want to pour it over your cereal.

(HE hands Andrew a bowl and a spoon. ANDREW watches Edward eat.)

ANDREW. Why are you still here?

EDWARD. I don't know. Why are you still here?

ANDREW. I'm still here because you wouldn't leave.

EDWARD. Well, I'm still here because you wouldn't leave.

ANDREW. That makes no sense.

EDWARD. You seemed to think it made sense when you said it.

ANDREW. Edward—

EDWARD. What?

ANDREW. Just leave. This has nothing to do with you anymore. You've done enough damage. Leave.

EDWARD. *I've* done enough damage?

ANDREW. LEAVE! WOULD YOU JUST GET OUT OF HERE?

EDWARD. I'm not even going to even respond to that. You know why? Because I'm getting a little tired of verbally beating the living daylights out of you.

ANDREW. Oh, is that what you've been doing?

EDWARD. As a matter of fact, it is. You and I fight, Andrew. This is the basis of our friendship. We fight, I win, and you lose. And it's getting old.

ANDREW. I lose?

EDWARD. That's right, buddy. So just eat your cereal and keep your mouth shut, because—

ANDREW. Lydia.

EDWARD. Excuse me?

ANDREW. I didn't lose then.

EDWARD. That had nothing to do with you. I mean, I admit that Lydia dumped me, but by then we were both sick of each other. That wasn't ...

ANDREW. Wasn't it?

EDWARD. You didn't start seeing her until months after she and I ...

(HE stops himself. Looks at ANDREW who looks back, deliberate. Pause.)

ANDREW. Lydia didn't want to hurt your feelings.

EDWARD. At the time, Lydia delighted in hurting my feelings. I don't believe you. If you were sleeping with Lydia while she and I were still together, I would have known.

ANDREW. Are you sure about that?

EDWARD. You were sleeping with her?

ANDREW. Yes.

EDWARD. You fucking creep. Don't you have any principles at all?

ANDREW. Did you actually say that? Mr. I Could Rape You If I Wanted—

EDWARD. Don't change the subject! You were sleeping with my girlfriend! Christ, you're no better than I am!

ANDREW. It was your own fault!

EDWARD. You were sleeping with my girlfriend at the time she dumped me! I think most people would agree I was the one getting screwed!

ANDREW. Don't play the victim. No one is going to believe you.

EDWARD. Yeah, well, don't you play the good guy. That's getting a little hard to swallow, too.

ANDREW. You didn't want her anyway!

EDWARD. That's not the point! You were supposed to be my friend! Well, fuck you. Just fuck you. I don't owe you shit. I'm getting out of here.

ANDREW. Thank God!

EDWARD. (*Looks for his jacket, starts to put it on.*) You know, just for the record, I did all of this for you.

ANDREW. What?

EDWARD. Yeah, that's right. As you'll recall, when you asked me to give Georgie a job, all I knew was she was some wild thing with no experience at all. Didn't even know how to *type*. But I gave her a job because you asked me to. And then, okay, after that, I wasn't exactly great for a while, but—

ANDREW. Wasn't exactly great. Excuse me, wasn't—

EDWARD. But at least I figured out what was going on and tried to stop it! I mean, I realized what an asshole I was being and I, I, I decided to change and try to make up for everything. So—

ANDREW. Oh, please!

EDWARD. I got you up here! I got you to admit how you felt about her! I mean, at least I got you to stop lying to everybody. And maybe it didn't feel so great, but at least now you have a chance at a real life instead of some—whatever—with Lydia. So don't go whining to me about what a big bad wolf I am. If it wasn't for me you wouldn't have anything right now.

ANDREW. I don't have anything right now!

EDWARD. Oh, that is complete horseshit. I mean, get a fucking grip, would you? Georgie adores you. You adore her. And all you can do is moan and gnash your teeth! I mean, I realize that relations between the sexes are confused nowadays, but they're not *that* confused. When she gets back here, you should just take her in your arms and take her to bed.

ANDREW. Well, thank you for your advice, Mr. Sensitivity. Take her in your arms and fuck her. That's very delicate and perceptive of you.

EDWARD. Oh, for—Do you want her or not, Andrew? Because if you don't, I'll take her, and this time, you won't get a second chance!

ANDREW. Forget it! I'm not giving her to you again!

(THEY stare at each other .)

EDWARD. I can't believe you said that.
ANDREW .You said it, too.
EDWARD. Jesus. We really are a couple of assholes.

(THEY sit for a moment, thinking about what assholes they have been.)

ANDREW. I don't know what's the matter with me. I don't know who I am anymore.

EDWARD. (*Pause.*) You were sleeping with Lydia?

ANDREW. Just once. We both felt so guilty about it
she had to break up with you before we could do it again.
She was going to end it anyway.

EDWARD. I know. That was my fault. I completely
fucked up everything with her. (*Pause.*) Don't tell her I said
that.

ANDREW. Edward, she's probably never going to
speak to me again.

EDWARD. Oh, right.

ANDREW. What are we going to do?

EDWARD. I don't know. But I have this terrible
feeling that we're not entirely in control of this situation.

ANDREW. We never were.

EDWARD. Oh, sure we were. I mean, remember when
we could just blame everything on women? Not a specific
woman. Just, women in general. The whole idea of
women.

ANDREW. Women.

EDWARD. It was so nice. Just blaming everything on
them. We didn't have to think about anything. We didn't
have to fight amongst ourselves, unless we wanted to.
Because it wasn't our fault. It was women. Fuck 'em.

ANDREW. Fuck 'em.

ANDREW and EDWARD. FUCK WOMEN.

(*THEY laugh at themselves.*)

GEORGIE. (*At door.*) Well, that *is* lovely.

(*The MEN stand quickly. GEORGIE enters, carrying
clothes, a bag of groceries and a book. SHE wears blue
jeans, a sweater and her heels.*)

ANDREW. Georgie.

EDWARD. Georgie!

GEORGIE. I can't believe it. Are you guys going to torture me for the rest of my life?

ANDREW. We were just—

GEORGIE. I mean, what the fuck are you doing here? What the fuck is this? Well, fine. That's just fine. You think my whole life is your fucking property anyway. I guess it's no surprise to find you taking over my apartment. (*SHE crosses toward the kitchen, angry.*)

ANDREW. That's not what we were trying to do.

EDWARD. We were worried about you.

GEORGIE. Right. You guys probably spent the whole night deciding which one of you gets me.

ANDREW and EDWARD. No! No, no, no, come on ...

GEORGIE. You both are hopeless. (*SHE dumps things on the table.*)

ANDREW. Where have you been?

GEORGIE. I was at Lydia's.

EDWARD. I was afraid of that.

GEORGIE. Yeah, we had a great time. We listened to records. Smoked cigarettes. Had conversation. You know, she talked, I listened. I talked, she listened. Very different from what the three of us have been doing, I gotta say.

EDWARD. Aw, come on, Georgie, would you stop being such a pain in the ass? We're trying to be sensitive, we really are, and you're just—

GEORGIE. Oh, now you're sensitive and I'm the pain in the ass. I love that—

ANDREW. All right! Could we just not—do that, right away? I mean, could we just try to be civilized for—I don't know. Five minutes, maybe?

GEORGIE. Fine. The clock is ticking. Here, have a muffin. I'm going to make some tea.

(SHE hands a packet of muffins to Edward and goes to the kitchen. EDWARD concentrates on opening them. ANDREW whacks him.)

EDWARD. What?
ANDREW. Go.
EDWARD. Now? I want to find out what happens!

(ANDREW stares at him.)

EDWARD. Okay! I'll be in the bathroom.

(And HE goes, taking the muffins. GEORGIE reenters and looks around.)

GEORGIE. Where's Edward?
ANDREW. He had to go to the, uh, the bathroom.
GEORGIE. Sly, Andrew. Very sly.

(SHE takes more groceries out of the bag. ANDREW picks a book off the table. As HE speaks to her, SHE continues to move around the apartment, unpacking groceries, going to the kitchen, cleaning.)

ANDREW. What's this?

GEORGIE. *Pride and Prejudice.* Lydia lent it to me. She says it's about a bunch of girls and their boyfriends. I thought it sounded good.

ANDREW. So. You and Lydia got along.

GEORGIE. You always told me I'd like her. I mean, I doubt we're going to be best friends or anything, but you know. The three of us, we should all have dinner sometime.

ANDREW. I don't think that's going to be possible.

GEORGIE. Well, it's up to you.

ANDREW. That's not—Georgie, could you stop— could you stand still, for a minute? Please.

(HE takes her by the arm and holds onto her for a moment. THEY look at each other. SHE looks away. Careful, HE leans in to kiss her. SHE pulls away.)

GEORGIE. I don't think you should do that.

ANDREW. I'm sorry. Yesterday, you seemed to want me to do that.

GEORGIE. Yeah, well, things were different yesterday. I was kind of fucked up. I mean, yesterday, I was actually going to screw someone I didn't much like just to prove some sort of stupid point that I can't even remember what it was. It's the kind of shit I used to do all the time. You know? I'm just lucky Edward isn't quite as bad as I thought he was. Neither is Lydia. She's a very forgiving person. You should call her, right now. I bet she'd be really glad to talk to you.

ANDREW. What are you doing?

GEORGIE. I'm telling you. I think you better call Lydia.

(ANDREW and GEORGIE stare at each other.)

ANDREW. You're changing your mind? *(Pause.)*
You're going to do the decent thing and send me back to
Lydia, the wronged woman who you've come to respect,
even care for—

GEORGIE. I'm not doing this for anybody but myself.
I just can't take it anymore, Andrew. Between you and
Edward, it's like, you both want—it's always about what
you guys want. And I'm just like some thing just spinning
in the middle of it all. I can't even think, you know?

ANDREW. If you're saying you're confused, that's
fine. I'm confused, too. We'll work it out.

GEORGIE. I don't want to work it out. I mean, I'm
confused, but I do know I don't want to be this person you
keep trying to make me. I mean, all these things about me
that really bug you, they aren't going anywhere. Let's just
walk away from it, huh?

ANDREW. I finally decided to confront it! I can't walk
away now!

GEORGIE. Look, I'm never going to be good enough
for you.

ANDREW. You are good enough!

GEORGIE. There's always going to be something
you're trying to fix—

ANDREW. I wasn't trying to fix you! All I ever wanted
was to help you see what is here! What your life can be.
You needed to change; you said so yourself! And you did
change. Because of me. What did I do that was so terrible?

GEORGIE. Well, you did a lot of things that were
terrible. And a lot of things that weren't. And I did, too;

I'm not saying I'm perfect. A lot of the time, I'm just a fucking mess. Mostly, I'm a fucking mess around you. I mean, when I'm with you, I'm always thinking about how to please you. How to make you happy. And then I hate myself when I don't. I need my life back.

ANDREW. I love you.

GEORGIE. (*Pause.*) You really should call Lydia.

(Pause.)

ANDREW. Can I say one more thing?

GEORGIE. What?

ANDREW. I like your shoes.

GEORGIE. What?

ANDREW. I like your shoes. Actually, I always kind of liked them. They look good on you. You have nice legs.

GEORGIE. Look. I'm sorry, okay?

ANDREW. Me too.

GEORGIE. You did help me.

ANDREW. I know. (*HE exits.*)

GEORGIE. Oh, *fuck*. (*SHE takes her shoes off, throws them down, sits and holds her head in her hands.*)

(Pause.)

EDWARD. (*Off.*) Can I come out now?

GEORGIE. (*Pause.*) Yeah.

EDWARD. (*Appears, his mouth full of foam, toothbrush in hand. Tentative.*) How are you?

GEORGIE. Not so great. (*Pause.*) Is that my toothbrush?

EDWARD. (*Looking at it.*) Is yours the red one?

GEORGIE. Mine's the only one, Edward. This is my apartment, remember?

(SHE takes it from him and goes to the bathroom with it. EDWARD goes into the kitchen, gets a glass of water and rinses out his mouth. GEORGIE reenters, trying not to cry. SHE starts to put groceries away again. HE stands in the door of the kitchen and watches her.)

EDWARD. Here, let me help you.

(HE starts to take them from her. SHE does not let him.)

GEORGIE. I'm fine. I'm fine! (*Pause.*) I'm not fine.
EDWARD. It's okay, honey. Come on. I'll make you some tea.
GEORGIE. (*SHE lets him take the groceries.*) Look, you probably should go check on Andrew, I think he's—
EDWARD. I'll get around to him. I'm more concerned about you right now. (*HE takes takes the rest of the groceries into the kitchen.*)
GEORGIE. I hope he goes back to Lydia.
EDWARD. I'd say it's anybody's guess what he'll do.
GEORGIE. I really like her.
EDWARD. She's all right.
GEORGIE. No, she's kind of great and you have to stop running around telling everybody she's a vampire. It's not funny and you're a jerk, okay?
EDWARD. Okay.
GEORGIE. Okay.
EDWARD. (*Pause.*) That's a nice sweater.
GEORGIE. It's Lydia's.

EDWARD. I know. I gave it to her.

(HE laughs. SHE stares at him.)

EDWARD. Oh, come on. I'm just trying to lighten the mood here. It's funny in a way, isn't it? Well, okay, it isn't, but sort of it is. Never mind.

GEORGIE. No, you're right. It is kind of funny. You know, they were sleeping together before she dumped you.

EDWARD. Yes, I heard. Apparently, the whole world has heard. I don't know what the big deal is. It was only once.

GEORGIE. That's not what Lydia says.

EDWARD. What?

GEORGIE. Did he tell you that? It was only once?

EDWARD. How many times was it? Never mind. Don't tell me. I don't want to know. *(Cleaning, HE picks up her shoes.)* These shoes really are beautiful.

GEORGIE. I'm throwing them out.

EDWARD. Oh, don't do that.

GEORGIE. They hurt my feet.

EDWARD. They're very beautiful.

GEORGIE. Look, Edward—

EDWARD. Sorry. Sorry. Go ahead. Throw them away. Do whatever you want.

GEORGIE. Sorry. I'm sorry.

EDWARD. Hey, come on, I'll make you breakfast. What did I do with those muffins?

GEORGIE. Listen, Edward, thanks, but could you just take off? I mean, I didn't sleep much last night, and I'm beat.

EDWARD. Sure. You're sure you're okay?

GEORGIE. Yeah. I'm fine. I am. I'm fine

EDWARD. Good (*HE crosses to the door. Turns back and looks at her.*) So what are you going to do now? Move into a convent?

GEORGIE. (*Pause.*) I knew that's what you were after.

EDWARD. I'm just asking.

GEORGIE. I should have known. You got so nice, so nice and helpful and reasonable. That's a sure sign that you want something.

EDWARD. I never made any bones about that.

GEORGIE. This whole concerned mother act—

EDWARD. I am concerned.

GEORGIE. Yeah, I picked that up.

EDWARD. He is all wrong for you.

GEORGIE. Edward—

EDWARD. I just hope you're not having second thoughts.

GEORGIE. I am not getting into this with you, Edward.

EDWARD. We're already in it. Aren't we? (*HE smiles at her.*)

GEORGIE. Oh, no. (*SHE picks up one of her shoes and wields it as a weapon.*)

EDWARD. Come on, Georgie. I'm not the enemy.

GEORGIE. You sure about that?

EDWARD. Ninety percent.

GEORGIE. Edward—we don't have the most romantic relationship here.

EDWARD. Neither of us is exactly indifferent. Come on. I'm not Andrew.

GEORGIE. That much I got.

EDWARD. And I'm not talking about a one-night stand.

GEORGIE. I don't care what you're talking about—

EDWARD. Don't you think people can change?

GEORGIE. (*Pause.*) Yeah. Yeah, as a matter of fact, I do.

EDWARD. Then what are you afraid of?

GEORGIE. (*Pause.*) Nothing. I'm not afraid of anything. (*SHE throws down the shoe.*)

(*Pause.*)

EDWARD. Good. (*Pause.*) Okay. You decide. And you let me know. (*HE goes to the door.*)

GEORGIE. All right. All right. But if you want to try this, you gotta know, this isn't going to look anything like anything you've ever been in before.

EDWARD. I know that.

GEORGIE. I'm not kidding, Edward. I'm not playing any more of your games. I'm not taking anymore of your shit. This is on my terms.

EDWARD. Of course.

GEORGIE. One kiss. For now, that's all you're getting.

EDWARD. I accept your terms.

GEORGIE. Fuck you.

EDWARD. Yeah, fuck you, too.

(*THEY kiss. The kiss goes on for rather a long time. SHE pushes him away. THEY look at each other.*)

EDWARD. Now what?

GEORGIE. Now we—negotiate.
EDWARD. All right.
GEORGIE. All right. Make me an offer.

(BOTH start to smile.)

BLACKOUT

End of Play

COSTUME PLOT

ANDREW

Khaki pants
White T-shirt
Green T-shirt
Pink and white striped long-sleeved shirt
Purple long-sleeved shirt
Faded white sneakers
Glasses
Watch

GEORGIE

Blue suit (Jacket and skirt)
White blouse
Blue high-heeled pumps
Green tank top (over-sized)
Pair of men's shorts
"Lydia's dress"
Black sequined dress
Black pumps
Jeans
Pink sweater
Earrings (2 pair)

EDWARD

Armani suit
Green and white shirt
Tie

Shoes
Watch
Brown Armani shoes
Watch

LYDIA

White pleated skirt
White body suit
Blue rayon jacket
Shoes
Earrings

(Note: Lydia and Edward never change costumes)

Act I: Andrew wears khaki pants, white T-shirt, pink &
     white striped shirt, faded white sneakers. Georgie wears
     blue suit (skirt & jacket), white blouse, blue high heels.
Scene 1:
Cue: "Oh fuck" Georgie exits stage left and changes into
     "Lydia's dress"
Cue: "I must look stupid" Georgie exits stage left and takes
     off dress and enters stage carrying a green tank top
     wearing just a bra & slip. She exits stage left again and
     takes a pair of men's shorts off stage with her.
Scene 2:
During blackout between scenes Andrew changes into green
     T-shirt and purple long-sleeved shirt.
Georgie changes into black sequined dress and black spiked
     heels.
In Act II, Scene 2, after Georgie exits from stage she
     changes into jeans and pink sweater.

PROPERTY PLOT

ACT I, Scenes 1 & 2 (Andrew's apartment)
Work table
Work chair (armless)
Chair
Armchair
Telephone table
Plant
Reading lamp (practical)
Wastebasket
Window grating
Window blinds
Area rug
Bookshelf units
Stereo system
Stereo speakers
Clip lamps
Swivel chair
Computer table
Computer terminal/keyboard
Desk lamp
Side table
Table lamp
Shelf w/table dressing
Posters

Hand props (I-1)
Telephone
Book manuscript
Pencil cup w/pencils
"Stunt pencil" (Andrew throws at Georgie)

Assorted books
The Iliad (paperback, Georgie)
Cutting board
Knife
Dish towel
Red peppers
Mug of tea w/teabag

Hand props (I-2)
Bottle of scotch
Manuscript notes in folders
Pencil holder
2 Glasses
Briefcase (Edward)
Filofax (Edward)
Dish towel
Cutting board w/ cheese, cherry tomatoes, crackers,
    mustard
Knife

ACT II, Scenes 1 & 2 (Georgie's apartment)
Sofa
Afghan
Throw pillows
Armchair
2 End tables
Telephone
Table lamp
Area rug
Window drapes
Floor lamp
Bar unit

Knickknack wallshelf
Bracket bookshelf
Dining table
Dining chairs
Hanging lamp
TV stand
TV
"Boombox" tape player
Umbrella stand
Low bookshelf unit
Set dressing (books, boxes, tapes, bar dressing,
    knickknacks, etc.)
Novelty X-mas light strands
Waste basket

Hand props (II-1)
Glass
Scotch bottle
Shopping bag
Briefcase
Jehovah's Witness books & pamphlets
Cassette tapes
Glasses (2 scotch, 1 water)
Mug of tea w/tea bag
Box of tea
Washcloth
6-pack of diet Pepsi

Hand props (II-2)
4 Glasses
Wash cloth
Diet Pepsi

Shopping bag & clothes
Mug of tea
Bed pillow
Comforter
Cereal bowls
Spoons
Box of cereal
Grocery bags (plastic w/handles) (Georgie)
2 Bottles of water
Quart of milk
Box of tea
Pack of muffins
Toiletries
Toothbrush (Edward)
Toothpaste (Edward)

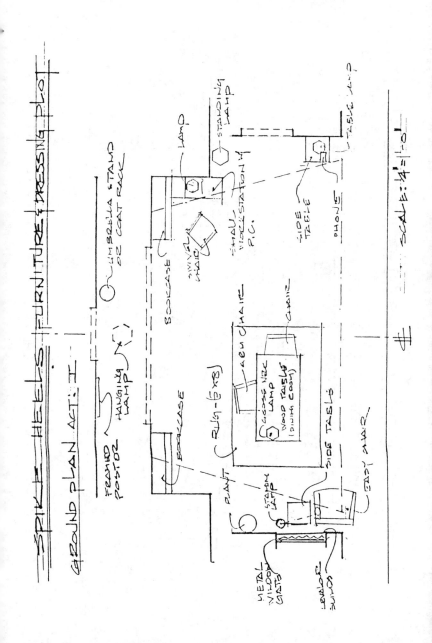

SPIKE HEELS FURNITURE & DRESSING PLOT

GROUND PLAN ACT. I

SCALE: 1/4"=1'-0"

UMBRELLA STAND or COAT RACK

HANGING LAMP

FRAMED POSTER

BOOKCASE

BOOKCASE

PLANT

RUG - (6'x8')

STANDING LAMP

BROWN NZG LAMP

ARM CHAIR

CHAIR

WOOD TABLE (DINING ROOM)

SIDE TABLE

EASY CHAIR

METAL & WOOD GATE

BUILDING EXTERIOR

LAMP

STANDING LAMP

SMALL WORKSTATION W/ P.C.

SWIVEL CHAIR

SIDE TABLE

PHONE

TABLE LAMP

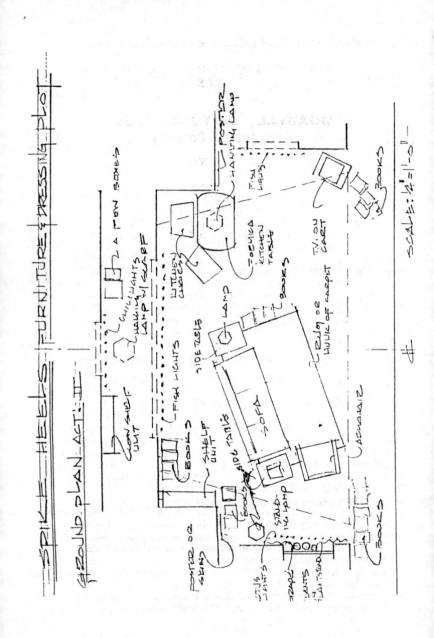

✔✔✔✔✔✔✔✔✔✔✔✔✔✔✔✔✔✔✔✔✔✔✔✔✔✔✔✔

OTHER PUBLICATIONS FOR YOUR INTEREST

COASTAL DISTURBANCES
(Little Theatre- Comedy)

by TINA HOWE

3 male, 4 female

This new Broadway hit from the author of *PAINTING CHURCHES, MUSEUM,* and *THE ART OF DINING* is quite daring and experimental, in that it is *not* cynical or alienated about love and romance. This is an ensemble play about four generations of vacationers on a Massachusetts beach which focuses on a budding romance between a hunk of a lifeguard and a kooky young photographer. Structured as a series of vignettes taking place over the course of the summer, the play looks at love from all sides now. "A modern play about love that is, for once, actually about love--as opposed to sexual, social or marital politics . . . it generously illuminates the intimate landscape between men and women." --NY Times. "Enchanting."--New Yorker. #5755

APPROACHING ZANZIBAR
(Advanced Groups—Comedy)

by TINA HOWE

2 male, 4 female, 3 children --Various Ints. and Exts.

This new play by the author of *Painting Churches, Coastal Disturbances, Museum,* and *The Art of Dining* is about the cross-country journey of the Blossom family--Wallace and Charlotte and their two kids Turner and Pony--out west to visit Charlotte's aunt Olivia Childs in Taos, New Mexico. Aunt Olivia, a renowned environmental artist who creates enormous "sculptures" of hundreds of kites, is dying of cancer, and Charlotte wants to see her one last time. The family camps out along the way, having various adventures and meeting other relatives and strangers, until, eventually, they arrive in Taos, where Olivia is fading in and out of reality--or is she? Little Pony Blossom persuades the old lady to stand up and jump up and down on the bed, and we are left with final entrancing image of Aunt Olivia and Pony bouncing on the bed like a trampoline. Has a miracle occurred? "What pervades the shadow is Miss Howe's originality and purity of her dramatic imagination."--The New Yorker. #3140

CEMENTVILLE
by Jane Martin
Comedy
Little Theatre

(5m., 9f.) Int. The comic sensation of the 1991 Humana Festival at the famed Actors Theatre of Louisville, this wildly funny new play by the mysterious author of *Talking With* and *Vital Signs* is a brilliant portrayal of America's fascination with fantasy entertainment, "the growth industry of the 90's." We are in a run-down locker room in a seedy sports arena in the Armpit of the Universe, "Cementville, Tennessee," with the scurviest bunch of professional wrasslers you ever saw. This is decidedly a small-time operation—not the big time you see on TV. The promoter, Bigman, also appears in the show. He and his brother Eddie are the only men, though; for the main attraction(s) are the "ladies." There's Tiger, who comes with a big drinking problem and a small dog; Dani, who comes with a large chip on her shoulder against Bigman, who owes all the girls several weeks' pay; Lessa, an ex-Olympic shotputter with delusions that she is actually employed presently in athletics; and Netty, an overweight older woman who appears in the ring dressed in baggy pajamas, with her hair in curlers, as the character "Pajama Mama." There is the eager-beaver go-fer Nola, a teenager who dreams of someday entering the glamorous world of pro wrestling herself. And then, there are the Knockout Sisters, refugees from the Big Time but banned from it for heavy-duty abuse of pharmaceuticals as well as having gotten arrested *in flagrante delicto* with the Mayor of Los Angeles. They have just gotten out of the slammer; but their indefatigable manager, Mother Crocker ("Of the Auto-Repair Crockers") hopes to get them reinstated, if she can keep them off the white powder. Bigman has hired the Knockout Sisters as tonight's main attraction, and the fur really flies along with the sparks when the other women find out about the Knockout Sisters. Bigman has really got his hands full tonight. He's gotta get the girls to tear each other up in the ring, not the locker room; he's gotta deal with tough-as-nails Mother Crocker; he's gotta keep an arena full of tanked-up rubes from tearing up the joint—and he's gotta solve the mystery of who bit off his brother Eddie's dick last night.   (#5580)

Other Publications for Your Interest

ALONE AT THE BEACH
(LITTLE THEATRE—COMEDY)
By RICHARD DRESSER

4 men, 3 women—Combination Interior/Exterior

"So you thought the kind of comedy that sends audiences home happy had disappeared from the American theatre scene? *Wrong!*" enthused the Louisville Courier-Journal over this literate, witty comedy, which had the audience at Actors Theatre of Louisville's famed Humana Festival whooping with laughter. George, a mild-mannered man in his mid-30's, has inherited a beach house in the Hamptons on Long Island. In order to afford to keep it, he has let out rooms to boarders, Manhattan-ites desparate to get out of the city on weekends. Blindly, and blithely, George has not actually *met* any of these denizens of the yuppie sector of the urban jungle. If everyone were Great Fun and Easy To Get Along With, everyone would have a great time—but the audience, of course, wouldn't. Who wants to watch a bunch of friendly, well-adjusted people have Fun In The Sun? Thankfully, Dresser gives us a motley crew of urban neurotics, male and female, who begin to drive George, and everyone else, crazy the moment they arrive. Somehow, though, everyone survives the experience, egos intact; and, in fact, some of the most unlikely romances develop, before everyone has to face reality: Labor Day and, subsequently, the trek back to New York City for good—until next summer? "Has a unique sparkle." New Albany Tribune. "A winner...a riotously funny sex farce."—Detroit News. "A charming romp that should turn up in regional and community theatres all over the place."—Houston Post. "Has the pacing of a Neil Simon script but with some of the dry, more cerebral wit of Jules Feiffer."—Evansville Courier.

(#3118)

EMILY
(ADVANCED GROUPS—SERIOUS COMEDY)
By STEPHEN METCALFE

8 men, 4 women, to play a variety of roles.
Bare stage, w/drops, wings, projections & wagons; or, may be unit set.

This brilliant, cynical, contemporary new comedy by the author of *Strange Snow*, *Vikings*, *Sorrows and Sons* and *The Incredibly Famous Willy Rivers* dares to take what amounts to a politically "incorrect" stance about the successful "New Woman." Emily is a successful New York City stockbroker who mixes it up with the boys and always comes out on top. In fact, she was described by one misguided critic as coming off like a "man in drag"; because, as we all know, women are caring, loving, nurturing creatures—and what a wonderful world it would be if *they* were in positions of political and/or business power, instead of those insensitive jerks, the *men*. Emily is just as cynical and ruthless as any man in her position; until, that is, she meets a caring, sensitive, aspiring actor (in other words, a nice guy with no money) who doesn't fall for her manipulative ruses; but, rather, for the real Emily he sees inside the ruthless yuppie—who may, or may not, exist. "Glorious...a sparkling comedy with bite to it. The title character is a gold mine of a role for an actress."—San Diego Tribune. "A real winner...a bravura balancing act right on the edge of sentimentality, finally and triumphantly crystalline in its emotional honesty...A triumph."—San Diego Union.

(#7076)

Other Publications For Your Interest

━ ▪ ━ ▪ ━ ▪ ━ ▪ ━ ▪ ━ ▪ ━ ▪ ━

PICTURE OF DORIAN GRAY, THE. (Little Theatre.) Drama. Adapted by John Osborne from the novel by Oscar Wilde. 11m., 4f., plus extras. I Int. w/apron for other scenes. English playwright John Osborne (Look Back in Anger, Inadmissible Evidence, The Entertainer) has given us a brilliant dramatisation of Wilde's classic novel about a young man who, magically, retains his youth and beauty while the decay of advancing years and moral corruption only appears on a portrait painted by one of his lovers. Following the advice of the evil Lord Harry, a cynic who, fashionably, mocks any and all institutions and moral precepts, Dorian comes to believe that the only purpose of life is simply for one to realize, and glorify, one's own nature. In so doing, he is inevitably sucked into the maelstrom of degradation and despair, human nature being what it is. "Osborne has done much more than a scissors-and-paste job on Wilde's famous story. He has thinned out the over-abundant epigrams, he has highlighted the topical concept of youth as a commodity for which one would sell one's soul and he has, in Turn of the Screw fashion, created a sense of evil through implication. Osborne conveys moral disintegration through the gradual breakdown of the hero's language into terse, broken phrases and through a creeping phantasmagoria."—London, The Guardian. "What is so interesting about John Osborne's adaptation of The Picture of Dorian Gray is that he had found in Oscar Wilde's macabre morality a velveted barouche for his own favorite themes. Osborne funks none of the greenery-valley vulgarity of the fabulous story, and conveys much of its fascination."—London, Daily Telegraph. State author when ordering.   **(#18954)**

FALL OF THE HOUSE OF USHER, THE. (Little Theatre.) Drama. Gip Hoppe. Music by Jay Hagenbuckle. 6m. 3f. Int. A comfortable suburban family man receives a desperate telephone call from an obscure and forgotten childhood acquaintance. Thus starts a journey into madness that will take Ed Allen to the House of Usher and the terrible secrets and temptations contained there. In this modern adaptation of the classic short story by Edgar Allen Poe, playwright Gip Hoppe takes Gothic horror into the 90s, questioning the definition of "sanity" in the same way Poe did in his day. Ed arrives to find Roderick in a state of panic and anxiety over the impending death of his sister, Madeline. As he tries to sort out the facts, he becomes tangled in a family web of incest and murder. Finding himself infatuated with the beautiful Madeline, his "outside life" fades from his memory as he descends to the depths of madness that inflict all the residents of The House of Usher. *The Fall of the House of Usher* is an exhilarating theatrical adventure leading to an apocalyptic ending that will have audiences thrilled. Actors and designers will be challenged in new ways in this unpredictable and wildly entertaining play. Cassette tape. Use of Mr. Hagenbuckle's music will greatly enhance the play, but it is not mandatory.   **(#7991)**

━ ▪ ━ ▪ ━ ▪ ━ ▪ ━ ▪ ━ ▪ ━ ▪ ━